Midge's round face lit into a grin. "A date?"

"A blind date."

"How exciting! Do you know anything about him?"

"Not a thing. But I've met her friends. They're. . .plastic. All polished and trendy and probably manicured."

Midge pressed her hands together in a prayer pose. "But she wouldn't set you up with a non-Christian."

"No, she wouldn't. But believers in Jesus come in many shapes and sizes. Red and yellow, black and white, real and plastic or uptight. . .you remember, you taught me the song."

Midge laughed then stood. She had a knack for never responding to sarcasm. "Well, stand up and let me get a picture. I'm not going to hang around and spoil Mr. Wonderful's first impression. I'll just lurk in the parking lot."

With a camera flash, a hug, and a giggle, she was gone.

In the silence, April found herself almost wishing Midge had stayed. She turned the recorder back on and finally remembered where she'd left off—her criteria for "Mr. Wonderful."

"I want comfy. I want a guy who enjoys the little things in life, like making a pizza and doing dishes together, or walking barefoot down by the river. I want a guy who doesn't try too hard to impress me. He listens to me and laughs with me instead of bringing me jewelry or flowers or—" There was a rap at the door.

April wiped her damp palms on the skirt of her polka-dot dress, took a deep breath, opened the door. . .and gasped.

Dressed in a black suit, white shirt, and black tie was Seth Bachelor. . .holding a mass of flowers. . .and a box of garbage bags.

A Wisconsin resident, **BECKY MELBY** has four sons and eight grandchildren. When not writing or spending time with family, Becky enjoys motorcycle rides with her husband and reading. Becky has coauthored several books with her writing partner Cathy Wienke for Barbour Publishing.

Wisconsin native **CATHY WIENKE** and her husband have two sons, a daughter, and two grandchildren. Her favorite pastimes include reading and walking her dog. Cathy has coauthored numerous books with her writing partner Becky Melby for Barbour Publishing.

Books by Becky Melby and Cathy Wienke

HEARTSONG PRESENTS
HP98—Beauty for Ashes
HP169—Garments of Praise
HP242—Far above Rubies
HP822—Walk with Me

Don't miss out on any of our super romances. Write to us at the following address for information on our newest releases and club information.

Heartsong Presents Readers' Service
PO Box 721
Uhrichsville, OH 44683

Or visit www.heartsongpresents.com

Dream
Chasers

Becky Melby and Cathy Wienke

Heartsong Presents

To Kristen, Holly, Adrianne, and Brittany. You are the women we prayed for before our sons were born.

Thank you. . .for accepting this family in spite of the Melby Wander and oyster stew, for not being Paper Dolls, but perfect fits for our boys, for adding stockings to our mantel, and for raising our amazing grandkids in the joy of our Lord.

I love you, Becky

To Nathan's beloved, Michelle Stempniewski-Wienke. I am so thankful to God for bringing you into our family. Thank you for loving our son. And to Brian's parents, Donald and Beverly Wienke. Thank you for raising my loving husband.

Love you all, Cathy

Thank you to Scott Emerson Crosby for sharing his water tower story. And kudos to Bill for creating the Polar Cap.

A note from the Authors:
We love to hear from our readers! You may correspond with us by writing:

Becky Melby and Cathy Wienke
Author Relations
PO Box 721
Uhrichsville, OH 44683

ISBN 978-1-60260-301-1

DREAM CHASERS

Our mission is to publish and distribute inspirational products offering exceptional value and biblical encouragement to the masses.

PRINTED IN THE U.S.A.

one

"I'm halfway to the top. No turning back now."

Gripping the rung tighter with her left hand, April quickly adjusted her hands-free microphone. "My knees feel like spaghetti, but I *will* do this." *Eighty-three, eighty-four.* She counted the rungs. *Don't look down.*

Her gaze followed the ladder to the point where the giant steel legs met the base of the water tank. She arched her neck, staring up—and up.

The ladder swayed.

Or had it? April's breath caught. Her heart hammered at her ribs. Hugging the ladder, she waited. "Vertigo. That's all it was. I won't do that again."

Her breathing slowed. She moved one hand and then her foot. "I wish this was television instead of radio so you could see the scripture verses I've written on the backs of my ha—" Her foot slipped. She gasped, heart pounding again, and regained her footing.

Rung by rung, she reached the base of the reservoir. The wind picked up suddenly. Her Minnesota Twins cap bounced against her forehead. Honey blond bangs pulled free and whipped across her eyes, blocking her vision for a moment and sending a fresh ripple of panic down her back. She focused on her hands. " 'I can do everything through him who gives me strength.' That's the verse on my right hand. On my left, I have—"

The whir of helicopter blades covered her words as a massive shadow blocked the sun, darkening the pale blue surface of the water tower and obliterating her words.

"Well, folks," she shouted into the microphone, "this is why the powers that be at KPOG don't let me do live radio yet!" It was a comment she'd delete before it reached the ears of anyone back at the station.

The helicopter rounded the water tower, giving her a momentary reprieve from the deafening vibration before appearing in her peripheral vision on the opposite side. "Looks like I'm not alone up here!" she yelled over the rhythmic pulse of the blades. The chopper hovered about thirty yards out. Afraid that turning her head would cause another wave of dizziness, she gritted her teeth and slowly looked to her right. . . directly into a camera lens.

The cameraman sat in the chopper's open doorway, his legs swinging in the air. Kneeling beside him was a man with a microphone. A man familiar to most of Pine Bluff, Minnesota—the local cable channel's weatherman.

Seth Bachelor. The sight of him made April's jaw tense and the cords at the base of her skull tighten like steel cables. Why him? Why now, in the middle of her first giant step away from fear?

But April Douglas knew how to hide her personal problems from the camera. She produced a TV smile. "The KXPB-TV news chopper is filming me."

Her hand grasped the rung that ran parallel to the bottom of the bright blue *i* in *Pine Bluff*. A catwalk with a railing circled the reservoir. She remembered this spot; she'd been here before, years ago. Here—but no farther. A siren and a blinding spotlight had stopped her.

The chopper edged away. The air calmed, and the noise dropped. But the helicopter hovered at a distance. "It's about time Channel Five decided to use me on camera." Another comment she'd delete before her show.

The presence of the helicopter messed with her train of thought. *Focus. Don't stop.* She moved to the next step. "The verse on my left hand is from Psalm 139: 'Where can I go from your Spirit? Where can I flee from your presence? If I go up to the heavens, you are there.'"

Reading the verse out loud acted like an intravenous drip of boldness, giving her just enough courage to let go with one hand and aim a smooth, controlled parade wave at the camera. For all her fears, performing on camera was not one of them. This was, after all, a chance to show KXPB-TV her versatility and make them sorry they didn't snap her up when they had the chance.

Strength seeped back into her legs, and her hands gripped the rungs with a determination that banished much of her anxiety. It all worked together to propel her faster up the vertical side of the tank to the point where the steel curved toward the top and she had to crawl. The metal rungs bit into her knees, and she couldn't shake the realization that only a skin of steel separated her from three hundred thousand gallons of water—and nothing but air separated her from the ground, 148 feet below.

Don't look down. She kept her eyes on her hands until she reached the last rung. A lightning rod marked the summit.

"I'm at the top! I made it!"

She'd expected to feel nothing but triumph and exhilaration. But instead, an almost palpable sense of aloneness engulfed her. She wasn't supposed to do this alone.

But she had. In spite of her fear of heights, in spite of the fact that her sister wasn't with her, she'd reached the top.

Just like she'd promised.

With a sigh that vibrated the windscreen on her microphone, she smiled. A tear dropped from her chin to the sky blue metal. Slowly releasing her right hand from the rung, she gripped the bill of her cap, pulled it off her ponytail, and flung it into the air.

"This is for you, Caitlyn!"

❧

"After nine inches of rain in less than twenty-four hours, the Snake River has crested and is overflowing its banks." Seth Bachelor adjusted his headset as he peered through the helicopter window. "Several houses have—" Movement caught his eye. "Look!" He nudged the pilot's arm and pointed. "Somebody's climbing the water tower!" The guys at the station would hate him for the editing they'd have to do on his flood coverage, but this diversion could prove to be newsworthy.

Grappling with the latch on his seat belt, he squeezed through the space between the front seats as the pilot banked and circled the water tower. Over his shoulder, he yelled, "Get the police on the phone. See what they know." He glanced at his watch. The morning news wasn't quite over. "And call the station and tell 'em to get a reporter over here—stat."

In the back, Rick James, the cameraman, already had his lens trained on the tower. Seth turned off his microphone. "Is it a girl?"

Rick had the advantage of a telephoto lens. "Oh yeah. Most definitely."

"How old?"

"Can't tell. Probably teens."

A voice crackled in his ear. "Seth? Merv. Can you go live with this in one minute?"

"Sure can."

The attack of nerves surprised him. He could give a weather report in his sleep, but the metamorphosis from meteorologist to reporter wouldn't be smooth. He cleared his throat again, shouted a few instructions at Jay and then Rick, and said a quick prayer that his brain wouldn't freeze up.

"In spite of warnings from the police and increased fines, some things never change. If it's spring in Pine Bluff, Minnesota, kids will be climbing the water tower. They've been doing it for more than fifty years, and as the end of the school year and graduation approach, we'll see more incidents of this illegal and extremely dangerous—yet time-honored—tradition. What's unusual about what we're seeing here is that this young lady is more daring than most. She's climbing alone and in broad daylight."

Whoever she was, she was in for trouble. "This girl's going to be arrested, and if memory serves me, the fine is likely to be around four hundred dollars." He stared at the girl's jean-clad legs and maroon jacket and the gold hair that whipped around her face. "She's halfway up the tank now. This is where we'd expect to see the spray paint come out, but she's still climbing."

A thought struck him. Was she going to jump? Sure, she'd just smiled and waved for the camera, but what if it was all a ruse? He leaned over Rick, getting a good look at the base of the tower. "There are a couple people on the ground watching her. One appears to have a camera or binoculars. I'm expecting police sirens any moment. . . ."

But what if the police were staying away purposely so as not to frighten her? Were they actually communicating with her somehow, trying to talk her down? Maybe it wasn't a camera or binoculars he'd seen after all. Maybe it was a bullhorn. "She's reached the top. I hope what we're witnessing is just a high school prank, but there's no way of knowing what her intentions are.

"I can't imagine what would bring this girl out here in the middle of the school day, knowing she's likely to get caught. I'm surprised that she didn't retreat when she saw our helicopter. You're probably coming to the same conclusion I am—there's a good chance this poor girl is climbing to the top of the water tower with thoughts of jumping. We've contacted the authorities, and you can rest assured that, if they aren't already down there trying to talk her down, they'll be on the scene any moment. Folks, if you believe in prayer. . .now would be a good time. This could be life or death."

"What in the world are they doing?" The chopper was closer now, the staccato beat of the blades so loud she couldn't hear herself think, much less transmit. How could a dinky cable television station like KXPB afford a helicopter, anyway? Slowly, she climbed back down to the catwalk. Standing upright, with both hands securely clutching the railing, she drank in the view for the first time.

For a moment, she was grateful for the excuse not to talk; no words came to mind. The panorama that stretched in every direction was a kaleidoscope of color. Flowering crab apple and cherry trees dotted the town like wads of cotton candy. The sky, cerulean and cloudless, seemingly washed clean by days of rain, met craggy bluffs to her left and white pines to her right. To the north, the brimming Snake River, true to its name, wound like an overfed serpent toward its junction with the St. Croix.

Nestled close to the banks of the St. Croix lay the town April was learning to call home all over again. Below the water tower, the high school football field spread out, surrounded by a cinder track. She'd run that oval more times than she could count. Looking down at the miniature runners, she could almost hear the crunch beneath their feet. She located the roof of her apartment and the house she'd grown up in, but when she attempted to find the steeple of her church, the chopper blocked her view. She glared at it, the same thought cycling through her mind again. *What in the world are they doing?*

If they'd hoped to see something dramatic, they must have figured out by now that she wasn't going to be performing any aerial stunts. They certainly had enough footage, though April was confident she hadn't done anything worthy of the six o'clock news.

Pointing to her microphone, she tried to wave them off.

What was the universal media signal for "I'm trying to tape here, you bozos!"? Maybe Seth Bachelor had all the time in the world, but she had a radio show that aired at three o'clock. If anything, her attempt at sign language made the helicopter edge nearer. Any closer and they'd rip into the reservoir. She could picture sliding down the newly created waterfall. *That* would be newsworthy. "Go away! Go do your weather thing!"

The catwalk was just wide enough for her to maneuver without turning sideways. She inched her way around to the west, hoping that News Chopper Five wouldn't follow her. As she took her third step, the helicopter rose straight up and made a beeline for the river. Silence echoed in its absence.

April drew a deep breath and tried to bring her thoughts back to her reason for being there. Switching on the microphone, she closed her eyes, needing a moment of introspection.

"So this is number one, the first thing on Caitlyn's dream list. As you can imagine, I'm experiencing a lot of conflicting emotions. By God's grace alone, I stared down one of my major fears. There's a sense of victory in that, but I can't help thinking how much fun this would have been with my sister leading the way."

The helicopter looked like a Matchbox toy as it followed the curve of the St. Croix River and angled west along the Snake. Sunlight glinted off the aircraft's side and on the brown and churning river below it. April swiped at another maverick tear. "But life goes on. . .and God has a way of turning tarnished dreams into something beautiful."

two

"You have *got* to be kidding!" April paced her living room, unable to share even a modicum of her best friend's amusement. "They aired it live?"

"In Technicolor." Yvonne Sondergard fluffed her white blond curls. "Couldn't really make out your face, but all of east-central Minnesota got a great shot of your Lucky jeans."

With a groan, April plopped her Luckys onto the couch but bounced up again. "What did they say?"

"They thought you were going to deface the tower. . .or kill yourself."

"What?"

Yvonne pulled a crumpled bag from under the coffee table and took out a tortilla chip. "He started out by saying that you were going to get slapped with a hefty fine when you were arrested."

Another groan emerged. "So everybody who recognized my backside thinks I'm in jail now."

"Yup." Yvonne stuck a chip in her mouth. "These are stale. You'd better make it perfectly clear at the top of your show that you had permission from the city and that the station would have taken responsibility if you'd plummeted to your doom. . .or leaped to your doom."

A twinge of guilt surfaced. "Yeah. . .about that. . .not so much."

"Huh?"

"Never mind."

"Seth was really getting into the drama of a possible suicide and—"

"Seth? You're on a first name basis with the weatherman?"

"Of course. I know the mailman and the crossing guard on the corner, too. What are you so stressed out about?"

"That man—" The phone on the kitchen counter rang. April sighed as she got up to answer it. Her quick trip home for a shower had taken half an hour so far, and she still hadn't had the shower. Her "Hello" echoed her frustration.

"April? I need you in my office. Now."

※

Jill Berkley's almost-black eyes smoldered. "Why?"

"Because the risk had to be real." April stood in front of her boss's desk, hands on hips.

"Did you even once consider the risk to the radio station? If you'd slipped, and landed in the hospital—"

"If I'd slipped, I would have splattered. There wouldn't have been anything left to hospitalize."

Perfectly manicured hands shot into the air above Jill's short-cropped black hair. "You're impossible!" Her sigh fluttered the papers on her desk. "April. . .you wonder why the board won't give you a live show, and then you go and pull something like this?"

"No one would have known I wasn't wearing a harness if that stupid helicopter hadn't shown up."

"So it would have been fine if you hadn't gotten caught?"

April shrugged. "Yeah. Sort of."

A hint of a smile pulled at the corners of Jill's mouth. "If you weren't so crazy good at what you do, you would have been fired months ago."

"So I'm not?"

Jill shook her head. "Once again, I went to bat for you. But you have to take this seriously, April. Three job applications have crossed my desk just this month. If you take too many chances, the board could run over me like a steamroller and hire somebody to replace you."

"I'll make it up to you."

"Make sure you do. Now go. Put together a show that will knock my socks off and make me forget all the rules you break."

April bowed, hands outstretched, grateful for the thousandth time that her immediate superior was far more friend than boss. She had her hand on the doorknob when Jill stopped her.

"That broadcast is on the KXPB Web site."

"Great." She stopped and turned toward Jill. "No, actually, it is great. I'll copy it and keep it as a reminder of my first big step. I'll just mute the commentary."

"Oh, you have to listen to it. It's highly entertaining. Seth Bachelor is layering the drama until his audience is convinced you're going to jump, and then all of a sudden there's dead silence, followed by, 'We've just received information'"—Jill's voice lowered to a rough impersonation of the weatherman—"'that this. . .woman. . .works for a local radio station. Evidently this is some kind of publicity. . .campaign.'"

"Publicity campaign?"

"Hey, he didn't say 'stunt.' Gotta give him credit for that."

April closed her eyes and leaned her head against the doorjamb.

"At the end of the news, they showed another clip of your climb and said, 'We now have the name of the lone climber.'"

" 'The Lone Climber.' Think I'll have a T-shirt printed with it."

"The timing was perfect."

"For what? Humiliation? I manage that on my own just fine." She ran one hand through hair still tangled in places from the chopper. "At least he didn't tape me throwing up when I got to the bottom."

Jill shook her head and tossed a mini Mounds bar at April. "They gave a plug for your show. That doesn't happen every day in the Christian radio biz. You may have a much larger audience today, thanks to Seth Bachelor." Jill flipped a calendar with the tip of her pencil. "And you can thank him in person next Saturday."

Bending to retrieve the candy bar from under a chair, April stiffened. "What do you mean?"

"At the citywide cleanup. He's the cochair, and you're interviewing him."

The wrapper on the candy bar in April's hand crackled as her fist clenched. "Get someone else."

"Why?"

"I've got. . .reasons."

"Well, get over them. You're doing the interview."

❧

"April?"

The flat voice coming through her office phone elicited a familiar wave of trepidation. April set her purse back on the floor and leaned against the back of her desk chair. She wouldn't be heading home soon.

"Hi, Mom."

"You should have warned me." A tiny, muffled sob finished her mother's last word.

For a split second, April considered playing dumb. But what was the point? "I didn't think you could get my show since you moved."

An empty space, filled with ragged breathing, followed. April closed her eyes, willing warmth into the cold spot in her chest. Too many guilt-inducing silences, over too many years, had leeched emotion from her soul.

"I drive up to the Goose Creek rest area on Saturdays to catch your show."

The picture of her mother sitting alone in her car, listening to her talk about Caitlyn from the top of the water tower, finally brought a twinge of empathy. "I'm sorry, Mom. I didn't—"

"I can't believe you're exploiting your sister's suffering like this."

Indignation rose like bile in April's throat. "How can you

think for a second that I would do that?"

"It's getting you closer to your goal, isn't it? My daughter, the next Oprah."

April's mouth jarred open, but nothing came out.

"Midge told me you were on the news, too." Her mother spat the words. "The weatherman—you do realize he's the one—"

"Yes. I know. I have to go, Mom." Without waiting for a reply, she slammed the phone into its base.

*

Over the next few days, the calls and e-mails generated by what the station employees were now referring to as "The Water Tower Show" lifted April's spirits from the pit her mother's call had left her in. Jill and the station owners were excited—the new kid on the block was having an impact. On a personal level, the e-mails stirred emotions that had just begun to settle. "Your words resonated in my soul," one woman wrote. She then went on to tell of her son's battle with leukemia. The boy had died just a week ago.

Resonate. That was the reason she'd gone to school—to make a difference in someone's life. But this level of public transparency was going to cost her something. On Wednesday morning, she was in the middle of a reply to the woman who'd lost her son when her phone rang. The young receptionist, usually poised and articulate, stammered over April's name. "I'm sorry. I know you're busy, but I didn't want to put this girl off. She's just been told she has an inoperable brain tumor."

Just listen and share your story. The advice had come from her grief support group. "I'll take it."

She listened. The girl was only sixteen, a year younger than Caitlyn had been. When the girl ran out of words, April spoke the one thing her sister had told her never to say again. "I'm so, so sorry."

"I love your idea." The girl's voice was hoarse with tears. "I don't want to spend whatever time I have left just thinking about dying. I want to live, like you said. . .to embrace life."

"That's a beautiful attitude, Libby. Are you going to make a dream list?"

"For sure. And the first thing on it is to lose my virginity!"

Lord. . .help! It was going to be a long morning.

❧

April recognized the boy with the wild swirls of light blond hair from a story she'd done on the Special Olympics. He was holding up a full trash bag as if it were a trophy fish.

"So why are you helping with Cleanup Day?" April held a microphone out to him.

"It's good to make the world cleaner. And I like the hot dogs. And the garbage bags are going to make a huge pile and get bigger and bigger and bigger like a volcano." He pointed to several volunteers in orange vests who were adding their bulging bags to a pile near the entrance to Founders Park.

Thanks in part to April, a picture of the finished "volcano" would make front-page news in the Sunday paper. She'd asked the city for permission to count the bags and estimate the weight. The director of the Pine Bluff Chamber of Commerce had taken her idea a step further and had arranged for all the bags to be dumped into a pile in the park where the volunteers would gather after the cleanup.

"Looks like you've worked really hard. You earned your hot dog." She switched off the microphone. "Follow that path to wash your hands first."

As she watched the boy's attempts to swing his bag to the top of the heap, she thought once again that she wished she were filming a television spot.

"Hey, if it isn't the Lone Climber!"

Yvonne's voice, coming from behind April, brought a smile. Taking in the three-inch heels, white skirt, and the lace that stuck out beneath Yvonne's mint green tank top, April shook her head. "You're a little overdressed."

"As if."

April laughed. The two words needed no explanation. Yvonne didn't own clothes for manual labor. She was a transplant from Minneapolis, having followed her fiancé to Pine Bluff just over a year ago. Like a hothouse plant exposed to the elements, Yvonne wasn't thriving well away from the city. She and April had moved in on the same weekend, meeting as they both carried boxes up the steps to their apartments above the chamber of commerce office.

Stretching her hands out, April threatened to hug Yvonne with her trash-picking gloves and was rewarded with a horrified grimace. She lowered her arms in a gesture of surrender. "What are you up to? Oh yeah, you're singing for a wedding in the Cities, right?"

Yvonne nodded. "It's an evening wedding, but I'm heading in early. The church is only a couple miles from Nordstrom's. Anything you need?"

"As if." As if she could afford even a pair of pantyhose from Nordstrom's.

"You doing okay today?" Yvonne gave her the kind of look most people reserve for stray kittens or children with skinned knees.

"Yeah. . .no."

"I've been thinking about you this morning, and I couldn't leave without seeing your face. I knew this was going to be a tough day for you."

A year ago, Caitlyn had roped April into helping with the cleanup. In her track uniform like the rest of her team, her sister had looked the picture of health, making it easy to deny her recent diagnosis. They'd talked nonstop as they picked up fast-food wrappers and soda bottles along the highway, laughing so hard at times they had to stand still to catch their breath.

As they'd stood in line for hot dogs, Caitlyn had made a

proclamation that would be forever etched in April's mind: "I feel invincible. I'm going to beat this thing."

And she had, for five months. And then she'd gotten caught in a thunderstorm, and two days after that she was in the hospital. A month later, April knew all the hospice nurses by name.

April shrugged and attempted a smile. "Thanks."

"Can I pray for you?" Without waiting for an answer, Yvonne placed a perfectly manicured hand, adorned with three silver rings, on April's arm.

As always, the words she spoke were poetic and cut straight to the heart of the emotions that pressed down on April like a physical weight.

Long after Yvonne left, her prayer remained wrapped around April like a warm shawl. Her friend was a contradiction in terms. A shopping guru who wore nothing but name brands, never went anywhere without makeup, and drove a bright red BMW, she also taught a junior high girls' Sunday school class and worked as program coordinator at the local nursing home. More than once, she'd literally given the shirt off her back to a resident who had admired it and gone home in a scrub top.

While the "material girl" image had never appealed to April, there was something about her new best friend that she envied. The girl knew who she was. Two years ago, April would have said the same thing about herself. Back when she was twenty-four and starry-eyed. Before her seventeen-year-old sister was diagnosed with leukemia. Before she'd left her job at the television station in St. Paul. Before she'd moved back to the town she'd waited eighteen years to escape.

"Describe yourself in one word" was something she said often in interviews. What word would fit April Douglas on this sunny April morning? Lost? To some extent that fit, but it made her sound helpless and pitiful. She was neither of those. If anything, she'd become stronger, not in herself, but in the knowledge that God could carry her through anything.

Before she found her one word, a girl about April's height, her hair in stubby pigtails, approached her. The girl appeared dressed for a rave instead of garbage duty. Multiple strings of shiny red and black beads hung over her orange reflective vest, and a tight black-and-white-striped shirt showed beneath it. April smiled. "Hi."

"Are you April?"

When April nodded, the girl said, "I'm Libby. I just wanted to say hey and thanks for inviting me to this trash thingy, you know? And I figured you'd want to know that maybe something good came out of all the bad with your sister dying and stuff 'cause I really did listen to what you said about staying pure, and I really do want to do something important with the ti—"

The sound of a motor in high gear stopped her words. April whirled around just in time to see a four-wheel ATV careening around the corner, heading straight for them. Whipping back around, she shielded Libby with her arms while yelling at her to move.

Missing her heels by inches, the ATV plowed into the mountain of bags. Paper and plastic debris exploded from the pile. The ATV slowed to a stop several yards beyond, leaving a wake of litter behind it.

Like a creature from a low-budget sci-fi movie, the driver, dressed from head to toe in black with a full-face helmet on his head, rose from the seat. With hands still on the grips, he half stood and turned. By then, April was within yelling distance.

"You could have killed that girl! You could have killed me! If this is your idea of fun, I can guarantee that you're not going to think picking up all that trash and rebagging it is—"

Black-gloved hands removed the helmet, and April stood face-to-face with the man she'd dreaded encountering today.

three

"Are you done?" Seth wondered if there was actual steam shooting out of his ears. "Because I'll just wait until you are, and then I'll explain that the brakes failed and I couldn't stop the stupid thing if my life depended on it—which it did! You're not the only one who could have been killed, lady!"

To her credit, the girl with the goldish blond hair looked appropriately mortified. She moved her sunglasses to the top of her head, as if needing to examine him better. As she stared at him, her expression evolved from anger to shock to embarrassment and then to the most artificial smile he'd seen in a long time. Strained though it was, he was pretty sure the corners of her mouth were pointed more up than down. Not that any hint of it was reflected in her eyes. They were pretty eyes—deep, deep blue surrounded by long lashes. She wasn't wearing too much makeup. Then again, she'd probably spent hours layering on the natural look. He knew from experience that the pretty ones were always stuck on themselves.

Maybe he'd come on a little harsh. He could take the high road here. "Are you two all right?"

The girl who looked like she was dressed for Mardi Gras nodded as she backed away, eyes wide with shock or fear, then turned and ran. The blond gave something closely resembling a nod. Wasn't this where she was supposed to ask how he was? *Your brakes? That must have been frightening! You're not hurt, are you? Should I call 911? Please accept my apology for completely spazzing out like that.*

"You're. . .Seth Bachelor."

Did the woman have lockjaw? Not only did she seem

incapable of an apology, she seemed to have trouble forcing words through her teeth. Was her mouth wired shut? Nobody could be that angry over a couple of busted trash bags. Who was she, anyway? Maybe she was the mayor's daughter and the garbage bags had come out of her allowance. He refrained from hurling that one at her. "I am. And you are. . . ?"

"April Douglas."

April Douglas. . .why did the name sound familiar? He'd remember that face if they'd ever met. Her eyes challenged, as if her name was supposed to elicit some response. He rifled through the little black book in his head. Sadly, most of the pages were blank. And if they'd dated even once, even years ago, he would have remembered those eyes. "Have we met?" It was the oldest pickup line in history; he hoped she wouldn't think that was his intention. She was absolutely not his type.

"Not exactly." Her tone was flat. "But I thought we shared a meaningful moment at the top of the water tower last week."

Oh no. Not her. *Lord, you do have a sense of humor*. Not sure what he was supposed to say, he opened his mouth, but she spoke first.

"Can I interview you?"

Interview? Ah. . .this was her way of getting even. She'd probably focus her questions on his qualifications for driving an ATV instead of his cochairmanship of Cleanup Day. Well, he wasn't going to make it easy for her. "Before or after picking up this mess?"

"During."

❧

April shoved a crumpled beer can into a filled bag that sat on the ground. "How long have you been cochairing Cleanup Day?" Head down, she didn't even look at the man in black as she held the microphone in his direction. If her equipment wasn't good enough to pick up his answers, she'd wing it with a summary of the interview.

"Three years. Gil Cadwell did it before me. KXPB-TV has been sponsoring the cleanup since the seventies."

If the leather jacket had buttons, they would have been popping. You'd think he was talking about running the country instead of garbage pickup. "*Co*sponsoring with the chamber of commerce."

He bent over, creating a tempting spot for April to plant her hiking boot. She reeled in the thought. Tossing a wad of newspaper into his bag, he turned, still bent over, and looked at her. "For the past five years, yes."

"But it was originally started by high school students. Yes?" Copying his word, she added her own inflection.

"No. It was started by the Kiwanis Club. They got the kids involved."

Did that little detail really matter? "I heard there were almost two hundred volunteers signed up this year. That's a bit of an increase over last year, isn't it?"

"Two hundred and three this year. Last year there were a hundred and eighty-seven."

The man was a master at splitting hairs. April stood, pressed dirty gloves against the small of her back, and stared at Seth Bachelor's hunched-over spine. "Who provides the food for the volunteers?"

"KXPB supplies the food and does all the recruiting of volunteers. The chamber of commerce donates the bags, reflective vests, and gloves." He stood up. One eyebrow crept a fraction of an inch higher than the other. "Your radio station foots the bill for the portable toilets."

That was it. April tied the top of a half-full trash bag. The toilet comment was the last straw. Not the fact, but the delivery. "Thank you, Mr. Bachelor, for your cooperation." Her bag sailed through the air, missing the weatherman by a good two feet.

❧

"You know him?" April handed a glass of sweetened tea to

Yvonne, who was sitting cross-legged on April's faded denim couch. "How come you never told me?"

"I did tell you."

"You made it sound like you knew him like you know the snowplow driver! You didn't say you *knew* him knew him. How come you never mentioned him?"

"It never came up. He's been in my Wednesday night Bible study for a couple of months."

"He's a Christian?" April didn't try to temper the incredulousness in her voice. "My sympathies to your pastor and his wife." After pouring her own glass of tea, she moved her giant white teddy bear to the floor and sat down on the other end of the couch she'd nabbed from her mother's basement before she moved. "The Larkins must have the patience of Job."

Yvonne's expression turned defensive. "Seth's a really nice guy."

Was she serious? Maybe Yvonne was just overtired from singing and shopping in the Cities. It was, after all, past midnight. April took a gulp of tea and a relaxing breath. Her emotions had been frazzled all day. She hadn't felt good about her show this afternoon and had spent the evening in a mental boxing match.

"Then maybe I met a different Seth Bachelor. I could hardly use anything he said in the interview. It was like he was deliberately condescending, and enjoying it. If I'd said the sky was blue, he would have said it was purple."

"And he would probably have been right. He's the meteorologist."

Yvonne's effort to lighten the mood almost worked. April gave a weak smile and stared at Yvonne. Was it possible she had more than a passing interest in Seth Bachelor? Yvonne was engaged, but until that license was signed, things could change. If that were the case, April shouldn't let her personal issues interfere. "Okay, so if he's not the obnoxious, argumentative know-it-all he appeared to be, tell me something good about him."

"He knows how to dress."

April's iced tea slopped over the side of the glass when she laughed. "You're right. How could I have been so wrong about the guy? His style sense should cancel out all the negatives."

"He's cute."

"A sad waste."

Yvonne lowered her head, staring through curled top lashes. "He's got a headful of Bible knowledge."

" 'By their fruit you will recognize them.' "

"He's really a nice guy!" Yvonne set her glass on the coffee table with a thud. In the silence that followed, a siren screamed below them, heading north on Main Street. "You just got off on the wrong foot with him. He's witty and deep and discerning— he's always got some new insight into whatever we're studying."

Where was his gift of discernment back in October? April sighed and rubbed her hand across her eyes. "Maybe he's got a Jekyll and Hyde thing going on."

Yvonne stood and took her glass to the sink, only ten feet from the couch in the small apartment. "I have to get some sleep." Putting her hands on her hips, she turned to face April. "Come to Bible study with me on Wednesday."

April picked up the white four-foot-high bear and plopped it on the couch next to her. Leaning against it, she curled her feet beneath her. "I have to wash my hair that night."

❧

She should have gone to bed. But Snow Bear made an inviting pillow, and she hadn't had the energy to move after Yvonne left. Now, squinting at the time on the microwave in the tiny alcove known as her kitchen, April massaged the kink in her neck. It was 2:32. Two hours of heavy, dreamless sleep in the fetal position and now she was awake, but her right leg wasn't. Dragging herself off the couch, she shook the pins and needles out. Her numb foot slid on something, and she looked down.

Her orange vest from the cleanup. Pictures of a day she'd like to forget flashed in her head.

Seth Bachelor was only part of the reason the day had gone wrong—she'd started the morning in a lousy mood. Grief was a strange thing. She'd been upbeat all week, buoyed by the positive feedback from the water tower show. Making arrangements for next week's *Slice of Life with April Douglas* had kept the adrenaline flowing and her time at the station busy. But from the moment she'd opened her eyes the day before, sadness had settled on her chest like a weighted vest.

Thoughts of Caitlyn permeated even the most inane details of her morning. Caitlyn writing "Happy Birthday, Ape" on the bathroom mirror with toothpaste. . .the food fight Caitlyn had started with scrambled eggs because April had used too much pepper. . .trying on wigs and turbans after they'd both shaved their heads before Caitlyn's first round of chemo. And then, reliving moments from last year's Cleanup Day and her sister's words, "I'm gonna beat this thing."

The way April had blown up about the ATV slamming into "her" pile of trash was evidence of her lousy frame of mind. Had she known who the driver was before she yelled, there would have been some sense to her outburst, at least in her mind. But the accident wasn't his fault. The brakes had failed, and he'd deserved some slack under the circumstances. It wasn't like her to go ballistic without first checking out the facts.

Yvonne's protective defense of the man was interesting. "Seth's really a nice guy." She'd said it twice. April had been in a miserable mood at the cleanup, but that didn't explain his bristling responses to her questions. So where was the truth in all the contradictions? Was Seth Bachelor a chameleon, showing his "nice guy" side only when it fit his purposes? Maybe she should show up at the Wednesday night study after all. . .seeing the other side would be fascinating.

Then again, maybe she should just wash her hair.

⋙

A low and distant rumble woke April to semiconsciousness. Pale pink light seeped between the slats of her blinds. Dawn. Sunday. What was the rumble? Her eyes shot open; her hand groped toward the nightstand where her cell phone quivered against the alarm clock. "Hello?"

"April? It's Jill. Sorry to wake you. I'm wondering if you'd be willing to do a live coverage."

"Sure. What is it?"

"Two kids from the high school were in a car accident last night. One of them was killed; the other's in critical condition. Some of the students are holding a prayer vigil outside the hospital. Orlando's going to cover the press conference with the highway patrol; I don't have anyone else who can go to the hospital."

"I can do it. Do you have the names of the kids?"

"Yeah. . .here somewhere. . .Dave Martin was the one who was killed. Brock Louis is the one in the hospital."

"Oh, no." Her heart skipped a beat. She sat up, throwing off the covers.

"April? Do you know them?"

"Brock was a friend of my sister's. How bad is he?"

"I don't have details. Critical is all I know. Can you do this?"

Her eyes closed, April lifted a prayer and took a deep breath. "I'll do it."

⋙

Six o'clock on Sunday morning. The streets of Pine Bluff were silent, though a few hours from now they'd be brimming with early season tourists in search of breakfast. As she pulled out of her parking space and into the alley that paralleled Main Street, April turned on the radio. She preferred silence this early, but knew she needed something to reset her mood dial. KPOG's six-to-nine slot was filled by Nick Joplin, an animated charismatic Christian who'd grown up in Warroad, just south of the Canadian border. Nick could talk faster than anyone April had ever met, though he didn't touch caffeine. "Got a Holy Spirit buzz going on," he claimed.

"It's 6:01 in beautiful downtown Pine Bluff. Daffodils bloomin' by my back door this mornin'. Just gotta praise God for color right now. Thank You, Lord, for all the little added touches. It's got its problems, for sure, but it's a fine world You made us. A fine world."

As always, Nick had her smiling in the first minute. When he played a praise song, she sang along.

Her 2001 Grand Prix knew the route from her apartment to the station and then to the hospital. How many times had she driven that circuit? But this wasn't the time to reminisce. *Lord, let me be a comfort. Let me respect their grief but find a way to share their story.* She turned the music up and sang until she got to the hospital.

She'd expected maybe a dozen teens. . .a small prayer circle near the front entrance. What she saw raised goose bumps on her arms. The grassy area inside the circle drive was full, not just teens but adults and young children. Fifty people, maybe more. . .at six thirty on a Sunday morning.

Father God, be glorified in this place. Let Your presence be felt.

ᴥ

There was something invigorating about Nick Joplin's voice. Seth wasn't the kind who needed three cups of coffee to get moving in the morning, and Nick's voice and choice of contemporary and gospel music fit his energy level. It was a good way to start a Sunday morning.

He was whistling to "Give Me Words to Speak" as he stepped out the back door and dumped an empty dog food can into the garbage. Just looking at the dark green bag that lined the trash can stopped the song on his lips. Trash. He'd picked up more of it yesterday than he'd touched in all of his twenty-seven years. He slammed the aluminum lid harder than he needed to and went back into the house, giving the screen door a shove for good measure. Maynard looked up from his chicken liver hash, reprimanding him for disturbing his breakfast.

"Sorry, boy." Seth ruffled the part-mastiff's ears. "That's what a woman'll do to you."

As he poured a cup of Highlander Grog coffee, his gaze landed on the flashing red light on the kitchen phone. Another reminder of what a woman could do. He'd looked at the caller ID when the call came last night but hadn't picked up the phone. The last thing he needed to hear at the end of a frustrating day was Brenda Cadwell's voice. As he knew it would, a text message on his cell phone had followed in minutes. His answer had been short and not so sweet.

Glowering at the annoying light on the phone, he headed for the bathroom where he turned on the shower radio along with the water, needing the music to keep his Sunday morning mind-set.

It didn't work. Thoughts of yesterday's fiasco flooded his mind. As if failing brakes and exploding garbage bags weren't enough, he had to go and have a run-in with that woman. Sarcastic, defensive, grating. . .April Douglas had been all that and then some. What was it about him that attracted the good-looking ones with attitudes? Where were all the soft-spoken godly women hiding out? And why was self-absorption so in style these days? He'd fallen for the queen of me-centered beauties, literally, and until he found someone who was everything Miss-St.-Cloud-wannabe wasn't, his last name would also describe his marital status.

The shower radio was still on as he wiped the steam off the mirror. Humming to the music, he looked down at the book on the counter, a commentary on the book of Romans. This morning, the adult Sunday school class at church would be studying the last half of chapter 12, the part about showing kindness to your enemies. If there'd been a way to get out of this lesson, he would have, but it was his week to facilitate the discussion. Once again, the thought hit him that God had a sense of humor.

Back in January, when he'd signed the clipboard, he had no idea what the topic would be this week. If the Christian Education Committee knew the extent of his hypocrisy, they'd show him the door.

Seth waited for "Sunday's Comin'" to end before reaching around the shower door to turn off the radio. As he touched the knob, Nick Joplin's voice changed, suddenly somber. "Two local teens were involved in an accident on Highway 65 around midnight last night. David Martin, a senior at Pine Bluff High School, was pronounced dead at the scene. Another senior, Brock Louis, is in critical condition at Emerson Memorial. April Douglas is live at the hospital where students have been holding a prayer vigil since word of the accident got out during the night. April, I understand you know the young man who was injured."

"I do, Nick, and I have to echo what I've been hearing from the people gathered here this morning. Brock is the kind of guy who never plays favorites; he makes everybody, teachers and students alike, feel. . .like. . . ," her voice faltered, "like a friend." Several seconds passed. "Dave Martin was one of those friends. He and Brock had been buddies since grade school. The kids, the faculty, and the staff are reeling from the loss. Allison Johansen was at the party Dave and Brock attended last night. Allison, I know it's not easy for you to talk right now, but can you give us some idea what Dave would want us to remember about his life?"

Seth stood, towel wrapped around his waist, fingers resting on the radio knob, transfixed by the tenderness in April Douglas's voice.

Maybe he'd been wrong about her.

four

Riverdance. . .at the Orpheum Theater in Minneapolis. She'd waited a long time for this.

April stood in front of her full-length mirror as she blow-dried her hair. On the back of the closet door hung the black dress with white polka dots she'd be wearing tonight. For once, she and Yvonne had agreed on a point of fashion—they were both wearing black and white.

Anticipation of Friday had carried her through a difficult week. She'd gone to the memorial service for Dave Martin on Thursday. She'd never met the boy, but neither had many of the twelve hundred people who had packed the high school auditorium and overflowed onto the football field. The senior class, Caitlyn's class, had filled row after row of folding chairs in the same space they would occupy at graduation just two weeks from now. Sitting in the bleachers, just as she had for so many basketball games, April had tried not to let her thoughts center on her own grief, but it had been an impossible task. In the third row, right behind Dave Martin's family, a single chair sat empty. Caitlyn's two best friends sat on either side.

As of Tuesday, Brock was in stable condition. April had gone to see him after he'd been moved from intensive care. When she'd held her hand out to him, he'd gripped it weakly and smiled through the tears that dampened his pillow. "Caitlyn's whipping Dave at one-on-one up there," he'd said. Through her own tears, April had agreed.

God has a way of taking our tarnished dreams and turning them into something beautiful. She didn't even know where that phrase had come from, but it was becoming a daily chant. She plugged in her curling iron and picked up her digital recorder.

"When Caitlyn and I ordered our tickets for *Riverdance*, we both knew there was a good chance I'd be going without her, but maybe the pretending gave her a few more days, or maybe it just gave her a little more to smile about in the"—the phone rang—"time she had left."

Snapping off the recorder, she lunged across the bed for the phone. "Hello."

"You know I didn't mean that remark."

Almost two weeks had passed since the "My daughter, the next Oprah" comment. April tucked the phone against her shoulder and picked a black bracelet from the jumble of jewelry on her dresser. This wasn't the time for confrontation. Nothing was going to undo the delicious anticipation of a night at the Orpheum. "How are you, Mom?"

"It's been a hard week."

"I know."

"Do you? Do you know what it's like when your only living daughter doesn't come to see you? Do you know what it's like when your ex-husband calls you out of the blue just to say you were a lousy wife?"

"Dad called?" Sickeningly familiar tension squeezed her abdominal muscles.

"Over a week ago. Not that you care."

Another too-familiar sensation took over. Her pulse picked up speed, and her ribs wouldn't expand enough to take in air. "Mom, I'll call you tomorrow. I have to go."

"You're getting ready, aren't you? You're going anyway, even without Caitlyn."

Fingers choking the receiver, April sank onto the bed. "Yes. I'm going anyway. I'll call you tomorrow." She hit the button that disconnected her from her mother.

Her hair was only partially curled when the phone rang again. The hoarse voice on the other end was only barely recognizable.

"Yvonne? What's wrong? Are you crying?"

"No." A coughing spell crackled through the receiver. "I'm sick."

"What? You were fine this morning!" April glanced at the clock, ashamed that her thoughts were totally selfish.

"I know. It came on so suddenly."

Sure of the answer, she asked, anyway. "Do you feel good enough to go?"

"No. I'm so sorry. But I found someone else to go with you."

April flopped onto the bed, facedown, talking into the spread. "I don't want to go with anyone else."

"I know, but you can't not go, and it would be no fun at all to go alone. Be ready at four, just like we planned. I made five o'clock reservations at JP's for dinner."

"With who?"

Another coughing fit erupted in her ear. She waited as Yvonne wheezed, sputtered, and gasped. "I think I'm going to throw u—"The line went dead.

&

She gave Yvonne enough time to do what she had to do in the bathroom and then walked across the hall. With a warning knock, she turned the door handle. It didn't budge. That was weird. Since theirs were the only two apartments and the door at the bottom of the stairs had a dead bolt, they rarely locked their doors. "Yvonne? You okay?"

Seconds passed, and then a weak voice said, "I'll be fine. Just the flu. I don't want you getting it."

"Can I bring you anything? I've got a can of chicken soup I can heat up."

"No. No foo—" The muffled sound of the bathroom door slamming covered her words.

By three thirty, April had worn a path in the berber carpeting between her bedroom and her front door. Dressed in the polka-dot dress and Yvonne's sling-back black shoes, she paced the living room, talking out loud to the two fish in separate bowls on a table beneath her front window. "She can't leave me hanging like this. Willy, you wouldn't do that to Splash, would you? Of course not, and you guys hate each other." Once more, she walked across the hall, heels clacking on the old wood floor. "Hey, I know you feel like death warmed over, but you have to at least tell me who I'm going with."

She waited, wondering if she could possibly have been heard over the sound of the movie on the other side of the door. She recognized the dialogue and Matthew McConaughey's voice. Yvonne was watching *The Wedding Planner*. Finally, the door opened, but only a few inches. Yvonne's pale face appeared in the crack above the brass door chain. "It's a date. Unlock the downstairs door and have fun." The door slammed in April's face.

за

This was not good. This was worse than not good. While Yvonne was engaged to one of the most charming men April had ever met, her taste in guy friends was not so great.

Halfway across the hall, a horrifying thought hit like a cherry bomb going off in her head. She wouldn't dare. . . . "Yvonne!" Backtracking, she pounded on the door. "Tell me you wouldn't set me up with Seth Bachelor!"

A weak laugh came from behind the door. "Huh. . .why didn't I think of that? You're so paranoid! It's Friday. Seth does the six o'clock news."

April's fist unclenched and slid along the door as an exaggerated sigh poured out of her.

But her relief was fleeting. Yvonne's New Year's Eve party came to mind in high-def. At least twenty of Yvonne's friends from the Cities had crowded into the tiny apartment April was now locked out of. True, she probably shouldn't have gone in the first place. It was just six weeks after Caitlyn died, and she wasn't up for a party. So maybe, just like last Saturday, her mood had colored her opinions. But still. . .her frame of mind hadn't influenced the main topics of discussion that night. Was brown really the new black? Did one really need live plants in each room to get the right flow of positive energy?

April unlocked the downstairs door, tromped back up to her apartment, shut her door with a controlled *click*, and proceeded to stomp her feet like a two-year-old. In the midst of her tantrum, her gaze landed on the black purse that concealed her digital recorder. She'd planned to record her impressions of *Riverdance* for tomorrow's show, but why not start now? Surely someday, she'd want to do a segment on blind dates gone wrong. Slipping the strap of her purse over her shoulder, she dug out her hands-free microphone, hooked the recorder at her neckline, and began to talk as she paced.

"My best friend feels sorry for me. She's never voiced that sentiment, of course, but I can tell. Case in point. . .when she suddenly came down with the flu today—today when we have tickets for *Riverdance* at the Orpheum—she set me up on a blind date with one of her friends. I've been looking forward to this day for months, and now, frankly, I'm scared stiff. I've met her guy friends. Please, no offense to any of you, but you're not my type. I love Yvonne dearly, but her criteria for friend picking are way different than mine.

"So what are my criteria? In my wildest fantasy, what kind of man would stand on the other side of that door when—" There was a rap on the door.

Wiping sweaty hands on her polka dots, April inhaled and opened the door.

"Ooh! Don't you look stunning!"

It wasn't her date. It was her aunt.

"Midge. How nice." April opened the door wider, expecting a lightning bolt at any moment. "Nice" had been a slight exaggeration.

"Just got back from the Cities. Your mom wants a picture."

Aunt Midge—all sixty-one round, overenergized inches of her—bubbled into the room. "Ooh. . .where did you get this?" She fingered the hem of April's dress, then, moving faster than her roundness should have allowed, she pulled at the neck and read the tag. "Ann Taylor. Wow. Expensive. But you deserve it, sweetie, and you've got the figure for it. Is Yvonne ready?"

"Did Mom actually say she wanted a picture?"

"Oh, you know. . . ."

"Yeah. How was she today?" No point in letting on she'd just talked to her and knew exactly how she was.

"A little better, I think." Aunt Midge unzipped the jacket of her three-shades-of-pink sweat suit. "We took a walk today, stopped for pie. . .and she actually ate some."

In the weeks since her mother had moved to Minneapolis to "get away from the memories," Midge's answer had never changed. *A little better, I think.* How many times had she heard it? April hadn't seen any improvement in her mother's clinical depression, in spite of a change in her medication and a new counselor. Leave it to Midge to find something positive.

Midge's cup was not just half full; it was eternally spilling over. But, as irritating as her effervescence could be at times, it was Midge's optimism that had stabilized her mother's downward spiral after Caitlyn's death, something April had been powerless to do on her own. Midge was one of those characters of whom people said, "You just gotta love her."

April managed a bit of a smile. "A daily dose of pie might do her more good than Paxil."

"It might at that. Is Yvonne ready?"

April sank onto the couch and lifted Snow Bear onto her lap. Her makeup kept her from burying her head in the long fur. Instead, she simply clutched him and groaned. "Yvonne's not going."

"What?" Midge dropped onto the cushion next to her. "You're not going alone, are you?" Her pink nails began making circles on April's back.

"I wish." She repeated the groan. "Yvonne set me up with one of her GQ friends."

The nails stopped circling. Midge's round face lit into a grin. "A date?"

"A blind date."

"How exciting! Do you know anything about him?"

"Not a thing. But I've met her friends. They're. . .plastic. All polished and trendy and probably manicured."

Midge pressed her hands together in a prayer pose. "But she wouldn't set you up with a non-Christian."

"No, she wouldn't. But believers in Jesus come in many shapes and sizes. Red and yellow, black and white, real and plastic or uptight. . .you remember, you taught me the song."

Midge laughed then stood. She had a knack for never responding to sarcasm. "Well, stand up and let me get a picture. I'm not going to hang around and spoil Mr. Wonderful's first impression. I'll just lurk in the parking lot."

With a camera flash, a hug, and a giggle, she was gone.

In the silence, April found herself almost wishing Midge had stayed. She turned the recorder back on and finally remembered where she'd left off—her criteria for "Mr. Wonderful."

"I want comfy. I want a guy who enjoys the little things in life, like making a pizza and doing dishes together, or walking barefoot down by the river. I want a guy who doesn't try too hard to impress me. He listens to me and laughs with me instead of bringing me jewelry or flowers or—" There was a rap at the door.

April wiped her damp palms on the skirt of her polka-dot dress, took a deep breath, opened the door. . .and gasped.

Dressed in a black suit, white shirt, and black tie was Seth Bachelor. . .holding a mass of flowers. . .and a box of garbage bags.

five

"Wow."

Shimmery, honey-colored hair fell softly. . .little black earrings dangled from her ears. And polka dots. . .they seemed to make a statement. Seth held out the flowers, knowing he was supposed to say something more than just "wow" but having trouble getting beyond that single syllable. This shouldn't be that hard. He talked for a living. "You look beautiful."

She appeared to be in shock. He couldn't decipher if it was good shock or bad shock. He held out the box of garbage bags. "I owe you an apology."

The color washed from her face. Her lips parted. "What are you doing here?"

He smiled, trying charm, though he wasn't sure he possessed enough to thaw April Douglas. "I'm your escort for the evening."

"No." She shook her head. "I can't. Not with you. It just. . ." Tears welled in her eyes. "No." The door closed.

Seth stared at the door, confusion tangling his thoughts. What had he done to deserve that? He'd picked up the garbage, and he'd apologized. What was wrong with the woman? Still clutching the flowers, he went down the stairs and out into the parking lot.

He was loosening his tie and debating whether he should throw the flowers under his back tire, when hurried footsteps made him turn around.

"Wait!" A short, forty-something woman dressed in pink toddled toward him. A gasplike sound escaped, and she stopped abruptly. "Oh."

He returned her wide-eyed gaze.

"Oh. . . ," she repeated. A sigh of apparent disappointment followed. "You're April's date."

"I was supposed to be. And you are. . . ?"

"Her aunt. Did she. . ." Her round face crunched into a grimace. "Was she really upset?"

Seth tilted his head to the side. "Yes, as a matter of fact, she was."

"Under the circumstances, Mr. Bachelor, I can't imagine you expected anything different."

"What 'circumstances'? Is she mad because I taped her idiotic climb up the water tower or because the brakes on my ATV failed? Neither are really criminal offenses. Does your niece have a habit of holding ridiculous grudges?"

The little woman's fingers flew to her mouth. "Oh," she said for the third time. "You don't know."

"Know what?"

The woman's top teeth pressed into her bottom lip. "Wait here."

Before Seth had a chance to wonder if he even wanted to, she walked away, disappearing into the building.

❧

"No."

April pulled the backs off her earrings and threw them at the coffee table.

"April Jean, the poor man doesn't have a clue what happened. You owe him an explanation for the way you acted and—"

"Owe him? I don't owe him anything. I owe Yvonne a kick in the shin with her own stinkin' shoes! I bet she's not even sick!" She dropped into her bentwood rocker. Midge knelt on the floor in front of her.

"This might be a step in the healing process." Her voice was low and soft, the voice that had whispered over April on so many sleepless nights.

"Maybe I'll talk to him sometime. Not tonight."

A gentle smile curved Aunt Midge's mouth. "You don't want to miss *Riverdance*. And it wouldn't be any fun to go alone."

"You'll go with me."

"I can't, honey. I have to clean the bank tonight. Yvonne would feel terrible for letting you down if you didn't go." When April didn't answer, her aunt picked up both of her hands. "Do it for Caitlyn, honey."

April pulled a hand free and wiped her face. "You do guilt as well as Mom. Only nicer."

"So you'll talk to him?"

Covering her face with her hands, April moaned. "Okay. I'll talk to him. But I'm going to *Riverdance* alone."

"I'll send him up." Midge got up from her knees, walked to the door, and exited, leaving the apartment door wide open. April listened to the downstairs door close and waited for the creak of footsteps ascending the stairs. A car horn blared from Main Street, a security alarm that wouldn't stop. The noise jangled April's frayed nerves. Her heart rate began to double-time. She didn't want to do this. Nothing she said would change a thing. April didn't subscribe to the idea that wounds needed to be reopened to heal.

The alarm stopped. In the silence, she heard the steps groan. In seconds, Seth stood in the doorway.

"May I come in?"

April nodded.

He set the flowers and the trash bags on the coffee table and sat on the couch. He rested his elbows on his knees and laced his fingers. Waiting.

Clasping her trembling hands, April took a deep breath. Staring into his eyes, the anger seemed to seep out of her, taking with it her strength. Weak and tired, she wanted only to crawl beneath the blanket on the couch. "Do you remember—last year—you took two high school students out to. . .chase a storm?"

He looked puzzled. "A buddy and I do talks to science classes on a regular basis, and several times a year, we take a couple of kids out with us. We're really just tracking, watching cloud formations, measuring barometric changes, not chasing. I'd never put kids in danger."

The anger returned, like starch to limp fabric. Every muscle in April's body tightened. "You put my sister in danger."

"What?" He leaned forward.

"Last year, in October, you took three kids out with you. One was my sister." Her eyes narrowed. "The one with the bald head."

Seth's hands separated, turning palms up. "I remember her."

"Do you remember getting caught in a hailstorm?"

A slight smile showed a dimple she hadn't noticed before. "Of course. But there really wasn't any danger. We were standing in an open field, no trees, no power lines. The storm hit us sooner than I'd expected, so we got wet, but there wasn't any lightning. The hail was small, and we made it to an overpass before it really started coming down. The kids loved it. We were all laughing hysterically." His hands lifted several inches off his knees. "There was never any danger."

April gripped the curved sides of the rocking chair. Her fingers bit into the wood. "Caitlyn wasn't strong enough." A picture of her sister's thin frame and pale face flashed in her mind. "Wasn't it obvious that she wasn't healthy?"

His lips parted then closed. He stared at her for several long seconds. "I thought she might have been anorexic, and she was wearing a hat, so other than how thin she was, we didn't know there was anything wrong with her when we first met her. Besides, that wasn't our call to make. We won't take a kid without a parental permission slip."

"What?" That wasn't the way April had heard it. She

started to say that her mother would never have given Caitlyn permission to go but stopped. What Caitlyn wanted, Caitlyn got. It had always been that way.

"What happened? She was fine when we dropped the kids off at the school." Seth's quiet voice interrupted her thoughts.

"She got pneumonia. She died five weeks later."

Seth's eyes closed for several seconds. He shook his head slowly. "I'm so sorry, April."

Once again, the simmering anger that had been a constant white noise in the back of her mind for so many months drained away. "It wasn't. . .like you said, it wasn't your responsibility." He didn't try to fill the silence. April was grateful for that. She stared at her fish, nose to nose in their separate bowls. "I've been a real jerk to you."

Seth smiled. "Hey, you haven't exactly seen the best side of me." His voice was soft and soothing, a voice more suited for late-night radio than a weather show. "We could make it up to each other by going to see *Riverdance*."

A jumble of conflicting emotions littered April's mind. Her mother had given permission for Caitlyn to go on the storm watch. Yet couldn't Seth and his friend have seen, just from looking at her, that she wasn't up to it? She thought of the way Seth had described it—Caitlyn running from the rain, laughing, breathless, thoroughly enjoying the moment. All this time, she'd silently accused those two men of taking Caitlyn's life. Caitlyn hadn't seen it that way, hadn't once placed any blame on them, nor had she ever expressed any regret for going along. Was it possible that they'd really given her something—a taste of real life, momentary freedom from the constraints of a disease that would probably have won eventually?

April stared at Seth, her answer to his suggestion changing with every tick of the clock. *You haven't exactly seen the best of me*, he'd said. She was seeing the best of him now, as he waited, nothing but concern in his eyes. But the other side, the one that had snapped sarcastic answers to her interview questions—how long would it be until she saw that face again? Thanks to her father, she'd experienced more anger in her twenty-six years than some people deal with in a lifetime. Her fear of it was justified.

Do not fear, for I am with you. . . . The Bible verse whispered over the tumbling thoughts. She'd climbed the water tower. She'd made a vow not to let fear run her life. If for no other reason, she could do this for Caitlyn. Looking up into dark eyes that seemed to say he'd give her all the time she needed, she ran her fingertips across her bottom lashes. She didn't want to miss *Riverdance*. And it was only one night out of her life. "I guess we could."

❧

Seth stood up, needing something to do while he waited for April to fix her makeup. He panned the small apartment, taking in details that gave clues about the woman who'd done the decorating.

Two round fishbowls occupied a small white table. In each, a single fish, purplish blue with deep red fins waving gracefully, floated near the top of the water, facing the other.

Over the worn blue couch hung a large framed photograph. He recognized it immediately. "Itasca," he said out loud. The headwaters of the Mississippi River. The picture showed a narrow stream dotted with rocks. In that spot, you could wade across the Mississippi.

April walked out of the bathroom, her mascara no longer smudging her eyes. Again, the word "wow" surfaced. He turned back to the picture. "I haven't been there since I was a kid."

"I love that place." There was reverence in her voice. "When I was about twelve, I wrote in the lodge guest book that I'd be back on my honeymoon."

"Douglas Lodge. . .any relation to you?"

"It was named for Attorney General Wallace B. Douglas, who was a great, great, great something of mine."

"So they should let you stay there free on your honeymoon."

April made eye contact for a split second. "By the time I was sixteen, my goals had changed. I wrote in the lodge book that I was going to become a park ranger and live at Itasca State Park. I actually took some classes in natural resource management before I switched to broadcasting."

Seth angled toward her. "What made you change your mind?"

"The money."

He laughed. "You forget; I'm an insider."

She smiled, but there was still something rigid about her expression. "Speaking of which, who's doing the weather tonight?"

"A friend of mine. . ." *My storm-chasing friend who was also with your sister in the hailstorm.* The thought brought the storm scene into focus again. He may have witnessed Caitlyn Douglas's last experience of enjoying life. ". . . a friend from college. He's filled in for me before."

April nodded, her eyes fixed on the picture. He studied her, only too aware of his lack of wisdom where women were concerned. His last relationship had ended much like the two Siamese fighting fish glaring at each other in their separate bowls. Opening both hands, he postured what he hoped was a peacemaking gesture. "I know we got off to a really bad start. . . ."

That wasn't what he'd wanted to say. Now he was giving the impression that he wanted to "start" something. "I'm really sorry about the whole water tower thing. . . . From now on, I'll leave the drama to you reporters." Her smile seemed real yet somehow guarded. He gestured toward the flowers and the box of garbage bags. "And I'm sorry about the garbage pile. The brakes really did fake out on me."

"I believe you."

"Could we maybe start from scratch? A whole new beginning?"

"I. . .guess so."

Seth extended his hand. "Hi, I'm Seth Bachelor."

She took his hand. "April Douglas. Thank you. . .for the flowers."

six

April glanced sideways at the profile of the man behind the wheel. He had a strong jaw. His hair was short but long enough in front to touch his eyebrow on the right.

He smiled, showing just a hint of a dimple. "I haven't had a chance to tune in to your Saturday show yet. I didn't want to hear what you did with that ghastly interview of me, but I heard your coverage of the prayer vigil. You're good. You don't come off as a vulture."

April laughed, surprised that she could. "I was a little more aggressive when I worked for WCCO."

"You've done television?"

"Mm-hm. Definitely my first love. Even tried to get a job at KXPB."

He turned, surprise covering his face. "When?"

"About eight months ago. I tried commuting from the Cities when Caitlyn started chemo. It was too hard, so I moved back."

"There must not have been an opening at the time."

"Oh, there was an opening, all right." She made no attempt to hide her feelings about the people he worked for.

"Who did you interview with?"

"Some guy with a potbelly. Sorry, I know you work for these people. He was nice about it when he called back to tell me I hadn't gotten the job. He said if it were up to him I would have been hired, but 'the man upstairs' thought I was overqualified and I'd probably move on as soon as something better came along. I don't think he was referring to God."

Seth's mouth formed what appeared to be the beginning

of "What" or "Why," but nothing came out. April jumped in. "Maybe we should talk about something else."

"Maybe. Tell me about your sister."

The green sign to April's right said they'd reach I-35 in eight miles. They had an hour drive ahead of them. If she was going to enjoy the night, she couldn't spend too much of it talking about Caitlyn. "She was diagnosed with acute lymphocytic leukemia a little over a year ago."

Seth's hand touched hers then returned to the steering wheel. "I heard you climbed the water tower for her."

April nodded. "She made a list." *When she was in the hospital with pneumonia.* Maybe it hadn't been Seth's fault, but would the thought continue to surface all night? "She called it her dream list. . .things we'd do together as soon as she was in complete remission. We both pretty much knew by then that she wasn't going to make it, but it gave us something to focus on instead of the disease."

"Now you're fulfilling the dreams?"

She liked the way he phrased it. "The day before she died, she made me promise that I'd at least try. It was her way of telling me to get on with life."

"And you're sharing your experiences on your Saturday show, I take it."

Again, his choice of words revealed a sensitive side. "I really struggled over that decision. I'm so afraid that people will think I'm exploiting my sister's tragedy." Her mother's words echoed in her mind. "But I learned so much from her. She made conscious decisions every step of the way. . .not to be fake, to express her anger but not be overcome by it, to accept the inevitable, and to make the most of each day. At a time when you'd expect depression and hopelessness, I saw her relationship with Christ grow into something I envied." She shifted in her seat to face Seth. "I think she'd want people to hear about her journey."

With a slight smile, he nodded. "I think you're right. What else is on the list?"

"This."

He turned toward her, confusion clearly registering. "This what?"

"Tonight. *Riverdance.* Didn't Yvonne tell you?"

"No." He was quiet for a moment. "Then we'll have to make this a very memorable night."

April reached down and picked up her purse, moving slower than she needed to. The night was already beginning to be memorable. Opening her purse, she pulled out a small notebook and a penlight. "Should I read some of it?"

"Some of it? How many things are there?"

"Forty-two." April waited for his reaction, and she wasn't disappointed.

His right eyebrow all but disappeared beneath a lock of brown hair. "Forty-two?"

"They don't all involve danger or expense."

He laughed. "But it sounds like you've got enough adventures to last for years."

Turning to the first page, April smiled, feeling wistful yet lighter than she had in a long time. "I hope so."

❧

"They aren't all huge adventures. A lot of them are pretty tame." She smiled at him. Her body language had transformed over the last few miles, and the more she relaxed, the more striking she appeared.

"Climbing a water tower is tame?"

"Compared to smuggling Bibles to Mongolia."

"Wow. I guess."

"Okay. I'll pick out a few things. . . backpack the Superior Hiking Trail, go rock climbing—indoor or out, visit the Grand Ole Opry, walk barefoot in the Rio Grande, ride motorcycles to the Harley rally in Sturgis, South Dakota. . . . We decided we'd either find cute guys to ride with or take lessons and get our own bikes."

Seth took a split second to ponder the wisdom of his next statement. "I don't know about the cute part, but I could help you out with that one. I've got a bike, and I've always wanted to do Sturgis."

"Seriously?" Her expression was wide-eyed and little-girlish.

Should he really give her hope of something he might not want to follow through on once he'd gotten to know her better? He couldn't quite imagine that happening. "Seriously."

"I've seen how you ride."

"Funny. Think you can handle ten hours on a Harley?"

Her chin lifted. "You keep the tires on the road, and I'll deal with the saddle sores."

The girl had wit. He liked that. "Ever ridden on one?"

"My boyfriend in college had an Ultra Classic. Unfortunately, I couldn't compete with the bike."

"Maybe if you'd started dressing in chrome. . . ."

Her laugh was so different from the wooden sound he'd heard earlier. "Why didn't I think of that?"

"What's next on the list?"

She turned a page in the notebook. "Have you seen the statue of Mary Tyler Moore at Nicollet Mall?"

"Of course."

"Caitlyn and I used to watch reruns from the *Mary Tyler Moore Show* together. So I took her to see the statue when it was dedicated in 2002. They gave everybody a tam, just like the one Mary throws on the show, but when it came time to throw them, nobody wanted to give them up. We kept ours." She was silent for a moment. "Caitlyn was buried with hers." Again, she took a moment, clearly having trouble steadying her voice. "Anyway, when we were making up the list, we came up with all sorts of places where we could throw hats. From the top of the Eiffel Tower or the Leaning Tower of Pisa—"

"Or the Pine Bluff water tower."

"Yeah. I guess it sounds silly."

"Not at all. Sounds like the stuff movies are made of."

"Hmm. . .it does." She flipped the page back again. "The next one is 'Watch the sunrise in Sunrise.'"

"Minnesota or Florida?"

Her head tipped to one side. "Minnesota. But maybe I'll add Florida."

"The sunrises might be a bit more spectacular. What's next?"

"Ride the jungle canopy on a zip line in Brazil, ride in a hot-air balloon, make homemade caramel corn and stay up all night eating it and watching Ashton Kutcher movies." Her hand did an elegant little flip. "See, they aren't all huge adventures. The next one, she put in to torture me, just like the zip line and the hot-air balloon and the water tower. I only have two major fears in life, and my sister hit them both."

"Fear of heights and. . .?"

"Storms."

He glanced at her, trying to read her emotions. Had she been afraid of storms before her sister had been caught in one? Was he inadvertently responsible for her fear?

She rubbed the palm of one hand with the thumb of the other. "Number twelve is chase a tornado."

Seth felt his pulse do a two-step. "So that was something your sister wanted to do?"

"Yes." She said it quietly. "I guess I should tell you. . . . While she was in the hospital after the. . .hailstorm. . .she said it had been one of the coolest things she'd ever done. She only wished she could have seen a tornado."

Clearly, that admission hadn't been easy for her. The realization touched him. "If. . .*when* you decide you're ready to cross that off your list, just let me know."

"Have you seen one? Up close?" He could hear the fear in her voice.

"Up too close a couple of times. Biggest adrenaline rush you could imagine."

"And you like the rush, I take it."

"Love it." Seth felt muscles on the side of his neck grow taut. If he didn't change the direction of this conversation, he'd be poor company the rest of the night. "Anyway, that's a topic for some other time."

"Okay, then let's change subjects again. What do you do for fun?"

Whether it was feminine intuition or her investigative reporter training, the girl had found the key to his egotistical heart. . .get him talking about himself. "Just about anything outdoors. Skiing, winter and summer, taking the bike out— year-round, as long as the roads are clear. I have a dog that takes me walking whenever he can. And I can be talked into cultured things like musicals and concerts on occasion."

"So tonight won't be too far out of your comfort zone?"

Seth ran a finger under his collar. "I'll admit that I much prefer jeans when I'm not working, but I'll dress up for a purty girl any day." He took his eye off the road long enough to enjoy the reticent smile teasing her lips. "What about you? What's a wild and crazy night out for April Douglas look like?"

This time she laughed, full and unreserved. "I read, I go to church—the same church I went to when I was two—I talk to my fish, and once in a great while, Yvonne drags me to the Cities where I reluctantly spend money on nonsale items. Wild and crazy are two words no one has ever accused me of. Well, not wild, anyway. Not yet."

"Mm. . .a hint of intrigue. The lady is mysterious, no?" His Antonio Banderas impression landed a little flat, but it did widen her smile.

"The dream list is my sister's final kick in the derriere. I've lived a very cautious life until now."

"Why?'

The question seemed to startle her. "Well. . .I guess I've got all the classic firstborn tendencies. Responsible, achiever, too sensible for my own good."

"Was it just you and your sister?"

"When I was five, my mom had a baby. He was killed in a car accident when he was six months old. It was my father's fault. My dad started drinking, and my mother's been in and out of depression ever since. Caitlyn was born when I was seven, and my dad left us two years later. . .the first time but not the last. There were times when I had to be the parent."

"There wasn't any chance for 'wild and crazy.' "

She shook her head. "I tried busting out of my mold once." Her lips pressed together as if trying to contain a smile. "That's when I climbed the water tower the first time."

"The first time?"

"My seventeenth birthday. My one day of teenage rebellion. I woke up that morning and decided I was sick of coloring inside the lines. So I called two guy friends who had climbed the tower dozens of times and told them to meet me there at midnight."

"And you did it?"

"Almost. One of the guys caged me. . .kind of like a human shield. It was all very exhilarating until I got to the catwalk and the cops showed up."

"Busted."

"Yeah. By my own father. He was making one of his rare guest appearances and heard me sneaking out of the house. He followed me and then called a friend of his who was on the police force. They took me to jail, and my dad sat and played cards with the officer while I sat in a cell all night."

"Ouch."

"Yeah. Some fathers might do that to teach a kid logical consequences. My dad did it for a good laugh with his buddy."

Something wrenched in Seth's gut. He had to fight the desire to grab her hand, touch her face, show her in some way that he understood. All too well. "And that was the end of your adventurous spirit?"

He shot a sideways glance at her, long enough to catch the funny little smile that twisted her lips. "I suppose it would have made some kids even more rebellious, but it just made me give up coloring outside the lines. But I've been pushing the envelope a bit at work lately, and I kind of like the freedom. I'm bound and determined to loosen myself up."

Seth stole another glance. "You're an inspiration. I could use a little coloring outside the lines myself."

seven

Magical. That would be the first word she'd record when she got home. The Celtic rhythms of *Riverdance* still reverberated in April's chest as the lights came up in the Orpheum Theater, and she stared at the massive brass chandelier dripping with Italian crystals that hung from the domed ceiling. From the mural above the stage to the rich Victorian colors of the carpet, the almost-ninety-year-old building whispered of its rich vibrant history. *Caitlyn, you would have loved this.*

April folded her playbill. "Can't you imagine being here back in the roaring twenties when it was all new?"

Seth nodded. "You'd be sitting there in a flapper dress, and we'd be watching the Marx Brothers."

"Did you know that Bob Dylan owned the Orpheum for a few years back in the eighties?"

"Really?"

She nodded. "The Minneapolis Community Development Agency bought it from him and renovated it in 1993."

Seth laughed. "You've done your research."

"I did a talk on it in college."

As she stood, Seth's hand touched the small of her back, light not possessive. "Thank you," he said softly.

She questioned him with her eyes. What was he thanking her for? The ticket? The company?

He answered, "You didn't have to give me a second chance."

The decision had been harder than he'd ever realize. But she had to keep the moment light. "It's hard to say no to a guy who brings garbage bags."

The shallow dimple on his right cheek creased. "Most guys

just don't understand how high trash bags are on a woman's list of priorities."

"You're very in tune."

"I try." He gave a comically exaggerated sigh as they stepped into the aisle. "Let's see how I do on the next thing on the itinerary."

"We have an itinerary?"

He nodded. "An incredible night deserves an extraordinary dessert."

❧

"Kuik E Mart?" April narrowed her eyes at Seth but couldn't quite tame the smile that seemed to be becoming a habit. "Our extraordinary dessert is coming from a convenience store?"

Seth winked at her. "I said 'extraordinary,' not 'gourmet.' Wait here." He opened the door then turned back to her. "One question. Strawberry or raspberry?"

"Surprise me."

He got out, walked up to the entrance, stopped, and came back to her side of the car and tapped on the window. April pushed the button to lower the window.

"One more question. You're not allergic to sodium stearoyl lactylate, are you?"

April's brow wrinkled. "I have no idea."

When he returned, he handed her two warm cups that smelled like hazelnut. She set them in the cup holders and took a plastic grocery bag from him.

"No peeking." He started the car and turned onto South Eighth Street. Five minutes later, he turned onto Cedar Avenue, and then Riverside, in the middle of the West Bank of the University of Minnesota campus. April knew the area like the back of her hand but had no idea what they were doing there. He parked in the parking garage just south of Locust Street. Picking up the two coffee cups, he smiled at her. "Follow me."

They walked across West River Parkway to a cement wall that ran along the riverbank. On the opposite side, the outline of the East Bank campus towered over the trees. Lights from the University Medical Center blinked in the darkness. Seth took the bag from her so that she could step over the wall. They sat, hugging paper cups of coffee, staring at the headlights and taillights strung like white and red beads on the bridge that crossed the black Mississippi.

After several minutes, Seth set both of their cups on the ground and handed April a roll of paper towels. "Would you mind opening these while I prepare dessert?"

As she ripped off the plastic, she watched. Out of the bag came two packages of Twinkies, a jar of raspberry jam, and a box of plastic silverware. Seth slathered jam over the top of a Twinkie and held it out to her. "Shortcake, madam?"

Closing her eyes, April savored the too-sweet concoction, all the while trying to put brakes on savoring the moment. "Delicious. And very creative."

"I invented it when I was eight."

"When I was eight, I lived on soda crackers and grape jelly." *Because my mother was too depressed to work, and my father wouldn't send the checks. . . .*

Seth gave her a thoughtful look, giving her time to add more. When she didn't, he filled the silence with stories of his childhood and tales of college misadventures that she was quite sure had been stretched. In between, he asked questions about her favorite memories but seemed to sense when he'd hit on something sensitive for her to talk about.

They talked about weather patterns and life in the media through two beeps of Seth's watch. "Midnight." He threw the Twinkies and jam back in the bag. "Don't want you dozing through your show."

April picked up the two empty cups. Instead of stacking them, she carried one in each hand as they walked back to the parking garage. Seth opened the car door for her and then walked around the front and got in. He held his hand out. "I'll take those."

She handed him the cups, fingers touching for a fraction of a second. As the dome light faded, his eyes found hers. "Are you busy next Saturday night?"

April's eyes opened, a little too wide, advertising that he'd caught her off guard. She needed time to think. Going with him tonight hadn't been her idea. Was she ready to agree to an official date? "No." The word in her head came out of her mouth, and she suddenly realized what she'd just done.

"Would you be interested in dinner and a truly gourmet dessert? The Melting Pot, maybe? Fondue for two?"

She had a whole week to make excuses. Maybe she'd catch Yvonne's flu. "That would be nice."

Seth's phone on the dashboard in front of her dinged. He reached for it. "Sorry. It's a message from my station manager. I have to check it." He listened to the message, his features hardening in the dim garage light. "Sorry," he repeated. "I have to call him back. He pushed a button. "Merv, what's up?"

The muscles on Seth's jaw bulged. The softness left his eyes. "Okay, so he was late, but he made it." His lips pressed together as he listened. "Hey, take it out on Darren; I'm not his nanny." His right hand slammed against the steering wheel. "When are you going to quit blaming everybody else for your problems? You should be able to deal with things like this without bringing them to me. And I'm not the only one who's taking notice. You'll be looking for another job if things don't start changing." April cringed as exasperation rushed through Seth's pursed lips. "You're a manager. Act like one!" The phone slapped shut.

❧

The magic was gone. The rest of the ride alternated between awkward silence and Seth ripping on the antiquated policies and woeful incompetence at KXPB, and what he was going to do to change things around there as soon as he had the chance. When he parked behind her apartment, April thanked him for the evening. After a quick good-bye, she got out before he could say anything. Locking the downstairs door behind her, she kicked off her shoes, sending one bouncing up to the third step, and trudged up the stairs. As she straightened up after picking up the wayward shoe, she shrieked.

Yvonne stood at the top of the stairs, wearing jeans and sandals and a turquoise blouse. Her hair was styled and her face made up. The overhead light glinted off her teeth as she grinned. "So?" she squealed. "Is he everything I said he was?"

April's eyes narrowed. "He's way too much of what *I* said he was." She opened her door and threw in her shoes. "Why aren't you in bed?" She took a long look at the bouncy curls and pearly pink lip gloss, the perky smile now phasing into confusion. "Why don't you look sick?"

"Because I'm. . .not. Didn't Seth tell you?"

"Tell me what? That my best friend's a liar?" She chucked her purse through the open door.

"He asked me to set up a date with you, and this just seemed perfect." Yvonne's disappointment pinched her features. "I was so sure you two would hit it off and you'd be so grateful that it wouldn't matter that I faked being sick. What happened?"

"You should be an actress. All that retching and gagging and. . ." April's breath came in short, tight gulps. One more word would unleash the torrent brewing inside her. With a final glare at Yvonne, she walked into her apartment and closed the door behind her.

The tears began as she unzipped her dress, clawing at the zipper as if it were the polka dots' fault she couldn't breathe. The dress fell at her feet, and she kicked it toward the closet. Jerking open a drawer, she pulled out a floor-length nightgown, pulling it over her head and hugging it close to her belly, seeking comfort in the softness. But the feel of flannel against her skin roused a sadness that had nothing to do with Seth Bachelor.

Arms wrapped around Snow Bear, she curled on the couch and gave in to tears. . .the sobs of an nine-year-old girl whose father had just said he was never coming back.

The tiniest details were branded in her memory, etched there by her father's rage: lightning flashing through the slats of Caitlyn's crib, striping the faded pink-flowered wallpaper. . . icy rain slapping the window. . .the wind howling, sometimes louder than her father's cursing, sometimes not. . . April had stood beside the crib in her long flannel nightgown, gripping the rungs, singing "The Itsy Bitsy Spider". . .louder and louder to cover the sound of the storm and the screaming in the kitchen. Caitlyn giggled, and April wondered why. Why wasn't she scared?

Looking back now, she knew the answer. Her little sister had never known anything else. She hadn't known a mother who smiled or a daddy who played games. To her, the fighting was normal.

April remembered the smoothness of the painted spindles, the fabric softener smell of Caitlyn's stuffed purple elephant, the hum of the vaporizer in the corner. And as hard as she'd tried to forget, she remembered her father's words, shot at her mother like the machine guns in the movies Daddy liked to watch. The connecting words had eroded over the years, but the bulletlike imprecations remained, shooting to the surface with unpredictable triggers. . .flannel—or a man's fight with his boss.

She hadn't seen or heard from her father since Caitlyn's funeral. There were times she could pray for him. Tonight wasn't one of those times.

Finally, when her tears were spent, April tried to back step into objectivity. Had she overreacted with Seth? Was she being unfair to let Seth's bout of anger overshadow the sensitivity she'd seen earlier in the evening? Maybe. She pulled a fleece throw off the back of the couch. Using the bear as a pillow, she lay down. Maybe she hadn't been fair, but she couldn't risk being around him long enough to find out. She couldn't risk falling for a man whose anger might burn out of control. A man who might leave her.

❧

"I know you had good intentions." April stared past Yvonne, counting the travel mugs on the coffee shop shelf, not quite ready for the honesty of eye contact.

"Does that mean you forgive me?"

In the fog of her exhaustion, even resentment felt like work. "I forgive you." The truth was, she felt betrayed, but she had to respond to Yvonne's motives, not the disappointing outcome.

"Then tell me every detail. . .everything before he got the phone call."

April shook her head. "If I do, you'll tell me I'm being irrational."

"And truth is something you no longer believe in?"

There were thirteen mugs on the top shelf, six stainless steel and seven plastic. "It's just. . .I don't know. . .he's not what I'm looking for."

Yvonne's just-waxed brows tapped her flat-ironed bangs. "Because you're looking for perfect."

"You're vicious this morning."

"Faithful are the words of a friend. Tell me about the rest of the night."

April stared over the rim of her Polar Cap, a frozen cappuccino concoction flavored with mint. "If I could blot out the last hour. . .he was amazing. I was determined not to like him, but I did. He asks questions and makes you feel like he really wants answers. He's interesting. He reads, he travels:

There wasn't a second of awkward silence. I was on the edge of my seat as he was describing hot and cold air masses crashing together." She rested the back of her head against the wall. "But my dad was a really nice guy a lot of the time."

"April...don't do that. Seth lost his temper—"

"Twice."

"Every guy gets frustrated with his boss. Don't generalize; don't make him into your father."

In the strained silence, Yvonne's phone rang. April counted bags of organic coffee while she eavesdropped.

"We're...I'm at Perk Place...yeah...sure...bye."

April opened a packet of sugar, sprinkling it on top of the half-gone Polar Cap. "That was short and sweet."

"Yeah. Just one of the girls in my study. Now, where were we? Oh yeah. We were talking about you generalizing."

"Let's talk about something other than my neuroses. What are you and Kirk doing tonight?"

"Dinner at his folks'."

"Name the kids again."

Yvonne laughed. An only child, she would soon be marrying a man with nine siblings, all with names starting with K.

Ten minutes later, April drained her cup and picked up her purse. "I have to get to the station. I was going to do my show on my experience at *Riverdance*." She sighed and crumpled her napkin, stuffing it into the paper cup. "Maybe I'll do it on changing weather patterns instead."

Yvonne didn't appear to have heard her last remark. Her eyes were focused somewhere over April's head, in the direction of the front door. Seconds later, a woman stood by their table, holding out a vase of tulips. The vase was surrounded by tissue paper...and sitting in an empty Twinkie box.

"April? This is for you."

eight

"I want to do a call-in show today." April stood in front of Jill's desk, hands on hips.

Her boss sighed. "We've talked about this."

"How come Orlando gets to do a call-in?" She played the whiny-toddler act to the hilt. "I've been here almost as long as he has."

"Orlando takes questions on hermeneutics. Your listeners are. . .diverse. . .'unpigeonholeable.' Like I said, we've talked about this."

"I know. I'm going to wear you down."

Jill threw a Mounds bar at her, hitting her in the shoulder. "It's not me you have to convince."

"But you think I could do it?"

"Of course. You know how frustrated I am that we're not utilizing your full potential. It's a liability thing with the board."

April bent to retrieve the candy from under a chair. "I happen to know they're meeting this morning. Do you want to get your name on the agenda, or should I?"

With a barely stifled laugh, Jill held both hands in the air. "I'll do it."

"Yes! Tell them it's just a trial run. And tell them my reaction time is like lightning. The slightest hint of anything unseemly and I'll hang up or hit the obscenity button."

"Okay, I'll talk to them. Get out of here and go work on Plan B, just in case my persuasive powers fail."

"Have I told you lately how awesome you are to work for?"

Another Mounds bar sailed her way. "Go. Pray. Don't waste

your silver tongue on me."

Licking chocolate off her fingers, April traipsed into her office and began typing her opening script. The idea had germinated, along with a headache, in the aftermath of her tears. Comments from her water tower show were still trickling in. Out of a listening audience that only numbered in the hundreds, April had heard so many stories of loss and hope. They needed to be told.

Several minutes into writing her opener, she stopped. A nagging thought, like a puppy scratching at the door, had pestered her since leaving Perk Place. *Riverdance.* She fingered a tulip petal, wondering half-consciously why she hadn't left them in the car. She'd told her listeners what she'd be doing on Friday night. She couldn't ignore it like it never happened. That, of course, was only a fraction of the thought. The rest, the part that concerned Seth Bachelor, she didn't have time to act on now. The flowers, and the note accompanying them, demanded a response. At the moment, she had no idea what it would be.

Redirecting her train of thought wasn't hard with the possibility of finally hosting the kind of show she felt God had designed her for. Or close to it, anyway. The real desire of her heart, the one she'd shared with only the people she trusted—the one her mother had thrown in her face after the water tower show—was a dream she'd probably never get close to.

Living in Pine Bluff, her chance of ever seeing her hopes materialize was beyond slim. All through school, she'd dreamed of becoming a television talk show host. Jill's comment fluttered around her as she worked. . .*we're not utilizing your full potential.*

There weren't many options open to her when she'd moved back home. One cable television station, and the nonprofit AM Christian radio station where she'd worked as jack-of-all-trades for eight months now. During the week, she was the afternoon disc jockey; in the mornings, she prepared for her Saturday show or played gofer for Jill. It wasn't a bad job, but it wasn't what she'd hoped for.

There'd been an opening for an anchor at KXPB-TV. With her experience, she'd been sure they'd hire her, but that turned out to be the reason she hadn't gotten the job. When they signed a girl just out of broadcasting school, April had been miffed. But maybe the "man upstairs" was right. There really wasn't any reason for her to stay in Pine Bluff now. Caitlyn was gone. Her mom was in Minneapolis. Maybe it was time to move back to the Cities where at least she had a chance of realizing her "full potential."

More than an hour later, she was engrossed in outlining her show when a hand jutted around the door frame. A slim-fingered hand with long red nails. It closed slowly into a fist, and the thumb popped up.

April squealed. "For real?"

Jill's slim silhouette slid into the doorway. "For real. I've convinced them you're the Christian radio version of Rush Limbaugh."

Two hours later, laptop under one arm, April was ready to head into the studio. As she switched off her desk lamp, a single tulip petal floated onto her desk. She picked it up. Red, with lines of yellow rising like sunbeams. She reached in her back pocket and pulled out the crumpled note that had been handed to her by Seth's delivery girl, the "girl from my study" who had called Yvonne at the coffee shop. She read the words that she assumed were handwritten by Seth. *"April—I had a wonderful time last night. I'm so sorry you had to witness that tiff. My invitation for dinner still stands. If you want to join me, just call W-E-A-T-H-E-R-G-U-Y."*

Lord, I will deal with this. I'll thank him. I'll forgive him. She tossed the note at the wastebasket and missed. *But I can't have dinner with him.*

❧

"This is April Douglas, and you're listening to *Slice of Life* on KPOG, praising our God in Pine Bluff. If you tuned in two weeks ago, you heard me talk about my sister, Caitlyn, and her dream list—forty-two things that she and I hoped to do together before the end of our lives. My sister didn't live long enough to experience even one of them." April took a sip from her Nalgene bottle. "Caitlyn Renee Douglas died of leukemia on November 12, but she made me promise to at least try to accomplish everything on her list.

"Keeping that promise is going to be possible because of the encouragement and help I'm getting from many of you. I've had offers of backpacking equipment, sailing lessons. . . ." April stood her gel pen on end and smiled. "A year's supply of Bridgeman's Wolf Tracks ice cream, and. . ." The words that came to mind weren't the ones she'd planned to say. "I even received an invitation to join a group of storm chasers tracking a tornado. And in return, I want to share my adventures with you."

She segued easily into *Riverdance*. She described the pounding cadence of the Irish jigs and reels, the sweet sadness of the violins, the refurbished opulence of the Orpheum Theater. Several times she used "we" but didn't mention who she'd shared the evening with.

"When the music ended, my first thought was how much my sister would have loved it. But. . .and this is the heart of why I don't want to keep these experiences to myself. . . my thoughts were bittersweet, not morose. I find myself remembering the good times and looking forward to whatever God has in store for me. Caitlyn's short life was a celebration. Even when she began to lose hope, she never lost her gratitude. I want my life to be a testimony to the wonder of God."

Her fingertip traced the edge of the keyboard. Though

she'd done a call-in show in college, this was different. "I've been blessed this past week to hear some amazing stories, some tender, some heart wrenching. Today, I'd like to give you an opportunity to talk. Grief is something we'll all experience at some time. We're called to 'Rejoice with those who rejoice; mourn with those who mourn.' Let's do that. Has the Lord led you through the valley and brought you out on the other side? What did He teach you there that might bring encouragement to someone who's still on that dark path? If you have a story to share that may offer hope, or if you're in need of some encouragement, the lines are open. . . ."

The first caller was a high school guidance counselor. "As most of your listeners know, April, Dave Martin, one of our students, was killed last week. He had a lot of friends, and it's been a horrendous loss for them. But these kids are doing some really constructive things with their grief. They're putting together a scrapbook of memories to give to the Martin family, and they've started a memorial fund; the money they collect will be donated to Habitat for Humanity."

An elderly woman called with a story of forgiveness. A year after her husband's death, God had finally given her the courage to face the woman whose decision to drive after too many drinks had cost her husband's life. The two women now met once a week for coffee.

A steady list of names filled her monitor through most of the first hour. The calls tapered off near the halfway point. April leaned in closer to the microphone. "On the other side of this break, I'd like to transition to a new topic. King Solomon gave us some wise words: 'There is. . .a time to be born and a time to die. . .a time to mourn and a time to dance.' My question to you is. . .are you dancing? Are you celebrating the gift of life? If not, why not? What's holding you back from rejoicing in the moment and embracing whatever God brings your way? I want to hear from you after this break."

April looked up to see Jill standing in the control room, once again giving the thumbs-up sign. April smiled her thanks and scanned the screen on her laptop, reviewing the cues that could keep her talking for the rest of the show if no one called in.

Three minutes later, she realized she wasn't going to need any of the cues. She welcomed the first caller. "Hi, Mary Jane. What do you have to share with us?"

"This may sound silly, but one of the ways I celebrate life is by completely ignoring all the rules of fashion."

April laughed. "I hope my best friend isn't listening. You sound like a free spirit, Mary Jane."

The laugh was returned. "Free in Christ. I'm in my sixties, and I'm a watercolor artist. I sell my greeting cards at craft fairs. So of course I love color, and I express that in everything I do, including what I wear. My neon paisleys and purple polka dots are a constant source of humiliation to my daughters, but you know what? I don't care! My grandkids love me just the way I am, and that's good enough for me."

"Mary Jane, you just keep on splashing color all around you, and maybe you'll give some of the rest of us the courage to do the same. Thank you so much for calling."

The hour went too fast. "We've got five minutes left—time for two more calls." She looked at the board. There were three names on the monitor. Frank, Carol. . .and Seth.

She had a choice. She pushed a button. "Hi, Frank. Welcome to *Slice of Life*."

"Thanks. I'm. . .glad I got through." The man sounded out of breath. "I've been listening to you on the last leg of a fifty-mile bike ride. I'm in my late thirties, and about a year ago, I took a long, hard look at my life. I was an overweight armchair quarterback, living vicariously through the flat-screen idiot box in my living room. So I did something that almost got me committed to a nuthouse."

April smiled and shook her head. All these fascinating people lived in Pine Bluff? "What did you do, Frank?"

"I donated my whole entertainment center to the Sanctuary Program."

"Wow! For anyone who isn't familiar with it, the Sanctuary Program offers housing and support for individuals and families in crisis. It's run by Pineview Community Church. Frank, you're an amazing guy. And what's changed in your life because of that decision?"

"I lost forty-one pounds, I've got a girlfriend, and I'm heading to Guatemala on a mission trip next month."

"Fantastic. Any advice to the armchair quarterbacks in our audience?"

"Yeah! God didn't create you to channel surf. Get off your. . . couch and do something purposeful!"

Two names stared at April as she said good-bye to Frank. With a deep breath, she pushed a button.

"Hello, Seth." There had to be more than one Seth among her listeners. "You're the final caller. What words do you have for us to end the show?" At least to her ears, her voice didn't lose a bit of its professional calm.

"Thanks for taking my call, April." Maybe there *was* only one Seth in Pine Bluff. Thankfully, nothing in his tone hinted that he knew her personally. "I've just recently been challenged by a friend's decision to color outside the lines more. I'm a pretty structured guy, but I'm excited about making some changes in my life."

April took a quick sip from her water bottle. "What kinds of changes are you going to make, Seth?"

"Well, for starters, next Saturday night I'm going to have chocolate fondue for supper. I'm all in favor of eating healthy, but sometimes you just have to skip the veggies and go straight for the cheesecake dipped in chocolate. So I've got reservations for two at The Melting Pot, and even if I end up eating alone, I'm going to enjoy coloring outside the lines. As far as final words, I'd just like to give kudos to the watercolor artist who called in earlier. The world could use a lot more polka dots."

nine

Pushing the door shut with one foot, April set her salad from Burger King on the kitchen counter. Her second Saturday call-in show had just ended, and she was still basking in the afterglow. The first had gone better than she'd dared to hope. In light of the positive feedback from last week's show, two members of the station's board of directors had called Jill, thanking her for "pushing for change" and "believing in that young woman."

She walked over to the fishbowls and pried the cap off the Betta food. "You two are looking particularly ticked off at each other today." She added a pinch of flakes to each bowl. "Didn't you guys listen to my show today? Life is too short to spend it mad at each other." A sudden stab of guilt scrunched her mouth into a grimace. "Do as I do, not as I say. Willy, you want to make a phone call for me?"

She'd put it off for a week, jumping each time any of her phones rang. Apparently, Seth was leaving the next move up to her. Thanks to his corny phone number, she couldn't claim she'd accidentally thrown the note away and lost the number. Staring at the clock, she reassured herself he'd be on set by now and not answering his phone. She dialed and listened, annoyed at the reaction his voice mail message had on her pulse. After the beep, she simply said, "Hi, Seth, this is April. Thank you again for the invitation, but I have to say no."

Feeling the nudge from her conscience turn into a shove, she hung up the phone. At the very least, she could have offered an excuse. Brushing off the thought, she took her salad out of the bag, threw away the plastic fork, and got a real one out of the drawer. She settled on the couch and was engrossed in *The Philadelphia Story* when there was a knock on the door. Yvonne, no doubt, here to bug her one last time about going out with Seth. With a resigned sigh, she paused Cary Grant and opened the door, salad in hand.

"Hi, sweetie!" Aunt Midge filled the doorway in a daffodil-colored sweat suit, holding two cups and her key to the downstairs door in her hand. "I met the girls at Perk Place and thought I'd bring you a Polar Cap. I know how you love those mint things." Midge handed her a cup and walked in. "Go ahead and eat your salad. I had a chicken salad croissant with Sue and Laura. Tried to get your mom to drive up and go with us. She always liked those girls, but. . . ." An impending frown suddenly morphed into a grin. "Maybe next time. I really came by to tell you that I loved your show today." Her gaze dipped to the floor. "Oh, that's not true. I just came by because I'm just dying to know if you're going to The Melting Pot tonight."

April held up her salad in answer and sat on the couch, gesturing for Midge to sit down.

"So you're eating a salad now and going out for dessert later?" Midge tilted her head to the right with a look of hopeful expectation on her face.

"I'm not going."

"Honey, you really need to give the man a second chance. . . or third, I guess. From what you've told me, he sounds like a sweet man who just had a little *LOGR* moment."

April's fork stopped in midair. "Logger?" Images of men in red plaid shirts floating logs down the St. Croix came to mind.

Midge giggled. "I just heard it at that women's thing I went to this morning. 'Lots of Grace Required.' Isn't that beautiful?"

"Yes. . .it is."

Midge's gaze went to the TV and then to the microwave. "The weather is on!" Midge scooped the remote off the coffee table and switched from DVD to TV. "I want to take my Sunday school kids outside tomorrow. I need to find out if it's going to rain."

Shaking her head, April flopped against the back of the couch. "That was lame, Midge."

"Shh. Listen to the weather." Midge pointed at Seth, who was perfectly filling out a tan sports jacket. "Look. . .it's raining dimples. . .and the sun is shining in those amazing eyes. . . ."

"Stop!"

"You're right. We should be listening." Midge turned up the volume.

April took a massive bite of lettuce, chewing as loudly as she could. But Seth's voice carried above her chewing.

". . .with Daisy Troop 401 this morning. I had the pleasure of answering questions about cloud formations." A video clip popped on the screen, showing Seth, sitting on a beanbag chair, talking to a circle of little girls. He held a microphone out to a five- or six-year-old with bright red hair. "What's your question, Pamela?"

The camera zoomed in on the freckled face and the crayon-printed name tag that hung around her neck. "My dad said that fog is just clouds on the ground; so how come in the sky, clouds sometimes look like kittens or turtles or something, but on the ground they just look like steamy stuff?"

Sitting at the little girl's eye level, the sleeves of his pale blue dress shirt folded back to just below his elbows, Seth smiled. It was, indeed, raining dimples. April stabbed a crouton and chomped, but she couldn't block out his answer.

"That's a wonderful question, Pamela. Wouldn't it be fun if there were cloud animals all over Pine Bluff on foggy days?"

The little girl nodded.

"Fog forms when the air temperature gets so low that it can't hold the water in it and. . . ."

April couldn't drown out the voice, and she couldn't keep her eyes off the screen. Seth's gentleness with the little girl was touching her in ways she couldn't ignore.

Midge turned the volume back down. "Laura's sister's daughter lives two houses down from Seth Bachelor, and Laura asked her what he's really like, and she said that he's just the perfect neighbor and—"

"That's what everyone always says about serial killers."

"April Jean!"

"Sorry."

"You are not going to find a perfect man, you know."

There was that word again. . .perfect. "I'm not looking for perfect. I just want a guy who doesn't have a hair trigger."

Midge wagged her finger. "Any guy with a pulse is occasionally going to lose it."

"I know. . .a LOGR moment." April set her salad on the coffee table, no longer interested.

"I'll make you a deal. If you go out with him, I'll clean your apartment for a month."

A moment of true temptation. A woman who cleaned for a living was offering to scrub her bathroom floor and chase her dust bunnies. April reached over and pulled her aunt into a one-armed hug. "I love you."

"I love you, too. Okay, if bribery doesn't work, how about guilt? I've heard you say that Caitlyn wanted you to do the things on the list because she wanted you to fully enjoy life. You know if she were here she'd be telling you to go for it."

April withdrew her arm. "You tried that once before. That's low, and that's so not like you."

Midge kept her eyes on her coffee cup. "I know. But sometimes the end really does justify the means. You've been moping around this dinky town with almost no social life for way too long. You need to practice what you preach. It's time for you to dance, my dear."

&

It's time for you to dance. Katharine Hepburn twirled, her calf-length skirt flowing out from her wasp waist. April pushed PAUSE and stared at the time on the DVD player. Seth wouldn't have left the station yet. *Lord, I need direction. The two people I trust most in this world are pushing me toward this man. I've always believed that there is wisdom in many counselors. Am I being overly sensitive? Is Yvonne right—am I projecting my dad's flaws onto Seth?*

Her eyes were drawn by a flicker of blue. Willy and Splash, in full battle mode, darted and dodged, their fins unfurled to intimidate. The threat seemed so real to them. April had separated them once, putting Splash on her dresser in the bedroom. But instead of finding tranquility, Willy had become hypervigilant, and Splash, if a fish can become depressed, appeared lethargic and melancholy. Though it was a love/hate relationship, they were good for each other.

Was the relationship between her Siamese fighting fish a metaphor for her life?

"Rrrrr!" She tossed the remote onto the couch. "Fine!" With a glare at her gridlocked Bettas, April picked up her phone. "Will you all leave me alone if I give him one last chance?"

&

To say he was pleasantly shocked would be an understatement. After a week of silence, her first message hadn't surprised him. Her second had almost knocked him off his chair. Seth stared at the girl in the teal blouse as he speared a maraschino cherry with a long, two-pronged fork and plunged it into the pot of melted chocolate. "So what are you going to cross off the list next? Salmon fishing in Alaska?"

A little divot formed at the right corner of her mouth. "I think you need to make your own list. I'm hoping to do a day hike on the Superior Trail in a couple weeks and something low-key this week. . . ."

"Sunrise at Sunrise? Minnesota, I mean."

"Hmm. . ." Pale light from the fixture above their table glinted in her eyes. "Maybe."

He chewed on his next thought for a moment before deciding to abandon caution. "I'll make breakfast."

April appeared to freeze mid-breath, like a kid in a spelling bee. *Could you repeat the word, please?* He decided to give her a way out. "Just a thought."

He pulled his fork out of the pot and slid the smothered cherry onto his plate. "You know, before we get onto something else, I want to explain about that blowup with my station manager." He'd already apologized—twice, if the flowers counted, but he wanted her to know it wasn't a regular occurrence.

April's shoulders lost their rigid lines.

Seth set his fork down. "Merv and I have a long history of getting under each other's skin. The guy's going to end up losing his job. He was out of line, but so was I. I apologized, and so did he. I'm just sorry you had to witness it."

"So this wasn't the first blowup?"

Now this was the thing—well, one of the things—he didn't understand about women. He'd just explained that he and Merv had said their apologies. Over, done, *finito*. Why did women have to dig things up and dissect them after they were dead and buried?

"We've had our disagreements. I've never lost it quite like that before."

"Obviously, you didn't lose your job over it."

Seth did everything in his power not to let his smile warp into a smirk. "No, I didn't."

April stared at him, as if wondering if he was worthy of amnesty.

Her silence made him antsy. "Maybe it's just a guy thing. I didn't waste any sleep over it. I'm pretty sure Merv didn't either."

Finally, she gave the subtlest of nods. "Everybody has logger moments."

"*What* moments?"

"LOGR. Lots of Grace Required."

"I like that. I pretty much constantly require lots of grace." He smiled as he watched April attempting to rescue a drowning piece of marshmallow that had fallen off her fork in the fondue pot. "You don't know how fortunate you are to be working with Christians."

"Actually, I do. I thank God every day for it." The blue-green stones in her earrings ricocheted light. Seth found it hard to stay disgruntled. He put the cooled chocolate-drenched cherry in his mouth.

Wrapping both hands around her coffee mug, April looked at him with an expression that reminded him of a nurse taking his pulse. "What are you doing in Pine Bluff?"

There were a lot of answers to that question, not all of which he was ready to share. "It's a friendly town. I like the energy during the tourist season and the slow pace in the off season."

April's eyes narrowed slightly. "Do you ever feel like you're not working up to your full potential?"

"I guess I don't need the big bucks to feel good about what I do, if that's what you mean." He set his fork down. "That sounded defensive, didn't it? I'm not really sure what you're asking."

"Do you ever feel stifled doing the weather on a little cable station when. . ." Her hand rose to her face, and she peered at him through spread fingers. "I'm sorry. That came out so rude." She dropped her hand to her lap and gave a sheepish smile. "I've been accused of projecting. I shouldn't be putting the junk of my life onto yours."

Seth's chest tightened. She couldn't possibly know her question had caused physical pain. "Then I should ask you the same thing. What's keeping you in Pine Bluff?"

Her eyes focused on the fondue pot on the built-in warmer between them. "I've been asking myself that question all day. My mother moved to Minneapolis last month. She was my reason for staying after Caitlyn died. I love the people I work with, but there's so much more I want to do with my life."

"Could you get your old job back?" Seth leaned against the back of his seat and folded his arms, wondering as he did what his body language communicated.

"Probably. But anchoring was really just a way to get my foot in the door."

"You have higher ambitions? Management?"

She laughed. "No." Staring up at the purple and green pendant light above their table, she said, "Promise you won't laugh?"

"Promise." Seth leaned forward, resting his arms on the table.

"I want to be a television talk show host."

He studied her, imagining her on set, her earrings and eyes flashing in the lights, asking probing questions. He reached across the table and touched his fingertips to the top of her hand. "You'd be good at that. Describe it for me: What does an hour on the prime-time *April Douglas Show* look like?"

The touch seemed to startle her, but she didn't pull her hand away. When she didn't answer, he filled the silence. "Big names, lots of controversial topics?"

Her honey blond hair swayed as she shook her head. "No actors, no politicians. For years I've pictured a show with a setup like Oprah's. . . ." She grinned and gave a one-shoulder shrug. "How's that for pretentious? I just mean a comfortable setting. No desk like *The Tonight Show*. And even when I'm nationally syndicated"—her smile was accompanied by a raised brow—"I'm only going to have regular people as guests. Real people with real stories of how God is working in their lives."

"Kind of like your radio show today."

"Exactly."

Seth brought his fingertips together. "Then make it happen, April." He looked down at the table then back to her eyes, not voicing the words in his head: *Would you consider starting small. . .say, at a "little" cable station?*

ten

The clock on the microwave glowed the hour. Four o'clock Saturday morning. An hour and a half before sunrise at Sunrise. April set her camera and digital recorder on top of the blanket in her oversize straw bag.

The only light filtering through the living room blinds came from the streetlamps below. April yawned and slipped a Vikings hoodie over her head. Carrying her hiking boots, she looped the handle of her bag over her wrist, opened the door, and stepped into the hall.

"This is getting serious."

April jumped at the sleepy voice. Whirling around, she laughed. Yvonne leaned on her door frame, wrapped in a purple satin robe, a towel on her head and lime green spacers between her toes. The smell of nail polish wafted through her open door.

"What in the world are you doing up?"

"Primping. I'm singing for a wedding in Edina at eleven." Yvonne's turban tipped to one side. "I heard about your sunrise breakfast. . .*from Seth*." The insinuation wasn't even close to subtle.

"I. . .was going to tell you." It was true. She was going to tell her. . .after the fact.

Yvonne's hands landed on her hips. "What did you think I'd do if you admitted you liked him? Do you really think I'm immature enough to say I told you so?" Even in the dim hall light, the bulge made by her tongue in her cheek couldn't be missed.

"Yes."

"You're right. I am." Yvonne stuck her thumbs in her ears and wiggled her fingers. "I told you so."

"Who says I like him? I need to cross this thing off my list, and he offered to bring food. Why would I turn down eggs and sausage cooked over an open fire?"

Yvonne laughed. "How many times have you talked to him on the phone this week?" Not waiting for an answer, she shook her head, waved, and stepped back into her apartment. The door closed and then opened just a crack. "I told you so."

❧

The purple LED lights on the dashboard of Seth's Camry gave just enough light to allow surreptitious peeks at his square jaw and the tiny bump at the top of his nose. April settled into the leather of the bucket seat. The outside-temperature display read fifty-four, but Seth had turned on the seat warmer before picking her up. Not really necessary but a nice touch.

Seth's right arm shot across her line of vision. "Moon's coming up."

"Just now?" April stared at the sliver of white nearly concealed by treetops. "It's almost dawn."

"As the moon orbits the Earth, it moves thirteen degrees eastward every night. Thirteen degrees translates into about forty minutes, so the moon rises forty minutes later each night. Once in a while, the sun beats it out of bed."

His look hovered thirteen degrees east of patronizing, but his words landed smack dab in the middle. It was the same tone he'd used to answer the little red-haired girl's question about clouds. April's fingers coiled around the seat belt shoulder strap. She could do patronizing.

"Wow." She batted wide-open eyes. "Is that a getting bigger moon or a getting littler moon?"

"That's a waxing crescent. After the new moon and before the full, it's called waxing. Like dipping a candle, it gets bigger—" He stopped suddenly, pressing his lips into a line. Slowly he turned, locked onto her eyes for a split second, and then focused back on the road. "I just came off like an arrogant snob, didn't I?"

April stifled a sneer. "What tipped you off?"

"I heard your teeth grinding." Smile darts radiated from the outside corners of his eyes. "I am so sorry." He flipped the right blinker and turned onto a narrow country road lined with tall pines. "It's my father's fault."

"What is?"

"The condescending attitude."

"Ah. It's in your DNA."

Tapping his foot on the brake pedal, Seth nodded. "It may be due to nurture instead of nature, but it's sure ingrained. You know that phrase 'Kids learn what they live'?"

Turning in the warm seat, April flipped the shoulder strap over her head and rested her back against the door. Maybe Seth Bachelor had way more in common with her than she imagined.

૱

"Tell me about your dad."

Seth was only too aware that she'd repositioned her entire body to face him dead-on. "Let's just say he was never satisfied with less than perfection. Because of him, I'm a TV weatherman instead of. . .some other things I could have chosen."

"Is your dad still living?"

Seth nodded. "My folks are in New Mexico. We see each other at Christmas and usually once in between. We get along fine that way."

His headlights bounced off a sign about twenty yards ahead. "We're here."

"Tippet House. A bed-and-breakfast?"

The quiver in April's voice made him smile. Clearly, she was questioning his intentions. "We're here for the breakfast part."

Her shoulders lowered. "I thought you were cooking."

"I am."

She didn't reply. He slowed to a stop in front of a Victorian farmhouse smothered in gables, cupolas, and gingerbread trim. Exterior lights illuminated pink siding and pale blue and white molding.

April's mouth parted slightly. "Are Hansel and Gretel here?"

"Let's go see."

They got out of the car, and he took her hand, guiding her along a winding brick path lit by ankle-high copper-shaded lights. The path led to the backyard, past a stone fountain. Water arced over the backs of two bisque-colored swans. Pink light shimmered through the streams.

April hadn't said a word since getting out of the car. Each time he turned to watch her expression, her eyes seemed to get wider. When they reached a gazebo aglow with miniature white lights, he walked up the first step. April stopped. "Seth. . ."

He suddenly realized that, aside from the radio show, it was the first time she'd called him by name. "What?"

"Thank you."

He squeezed her hand. "You haven't even seen the sunrise."

"I can't wait," she whispered.

He motioned for her to go ahead of him up the five steps. When she reached the top step, he heard a sharp inhale and smiled to himself. A round table, covered with a lace cloth, was set for two. Gold flatware flanked rose-covered plates and cups. Light danced from a three-wick ivory candle shielded by a hurricane shade.

Pulling a wrought iron chair away from the table, he gave a slight bow. April sat down, and he handed her a cloth napkin. "Breakfast will be served momentarily, ma'am." As he pulled out the chair opposite her, he heard steps on the brick walk.

Bessie, who had owned the Sage Stoppe restaurant before opening the bed-and-breakfast, ascended the stairs with a large silver tray. Tall and thin, with wisps of straight gray hair springing loose from a tight bun, she was as stoic as her Cornish grandmothers must have been. After resting the tray on a wooden stand, she set two covered serving dishes on the table, followed by a basket, the contents hidden by a linen napkin. With a nod of her head, she picked up the empty tray.

"I owe you my firstborn child, Bessie."

"That you do," she answered and disappeared down the stairs.

Instead of uncovering the dishes like he thought she would, April simply sat, smiling across the table at him. "This is not at all what I expected. You're a man of surprises."

"Is that a good thing?" It seemed to be. She was smiling, after all.

"Usually."

Reaching across the table with both hands, he turned them palms up. "Let's pray." When her hands rested in his, he bowed his head, grateful for a reason to hide for just a moment from those deep blue eyes. "Lord God, thank You for this food, and thank You for the witness of Your majesty we are about to see. Amen."

"Amen." Once again her lashes glistened, but she didn't appear in danger of giving in to whatever emotion was getting to her. She touched the edge of the napkin that covered the basket. "Don't tell me. Twinkies?"

Seth laughed. "Homemade biscuits."

As April lifted the napkin, a rose pink glow lit the cloth. Orange spears blazed through the eastern sky as the gold orb lifted from the horizon and gilded the valley below them with morning light.

≈

"Told you so, told you so, told you so. . ."

April sipped her Polar Cap as she listened to Yvonne's silly chant. Slurping on her straw, she stared, refusing to crack even the slightest smile. "That is so first grade."

The ditty finally came to an end. "But it makes me feel so good." Yvonne broke a scone in half and slathered it with lemon curd. "Details. Don't leave out a single second."

April toyed with the flip menu that displayed Perk Place's catering choices. She'd made Yvonne wait four days until their schedules would mesh so she could share the "details" face-to-face. A few more minutes would only enhance the anticipation. "Do you think any of the people in your Bible study would be interested in a day hike on the Superior Trail a week from Sunday? We could all go to the Saturday worship service at your church—"

"Ahem." Yvonne cleared her throat and held out her watch. "We have to be at Bible study in twenty minutes."

"Who says I'm going?"

"Hah! As if. You're going, even though it's for all the wrong reasons." She snatched April's cup, pulling the straw out of her mouth. "Details."

"He was very. . .creative." April recaptured her Polar Cap. "I imagined sitting at a picnic table eating scrambled eggs seasoned with ashes. But what I got was a candlelit table and *sformatino*."

"Is it contagious?"

"It means 'pie' in Italian. Kind of like quiche, full of veggies and cheese."

"And Seth made it?"

"With his own little hands the night before. The lady who runs the B and B baked it, but—" Her phone, sitting on the table, vibrated.

April stared at the caller ID screen and sighed as she opened her phone. "Hi, Midge."

Even before her aunt spoke, there was a sense of crackling tension in the silence. "April, why haven't you answered your mother's calls?"

A sigh started in the bottom of her lungs. There were four

missed calls on her phone since noon. "I couldn't find the time." *Forgive me, Lord.* She could have *made* the time. "She didn't leave a message. I was going to call her later. Is something wrong?"

"I've never heard her like this. She's so upset, and she's not making sense. Her words are slurred, and I'm afraid she took something. Should I call 911?"

April's mouth went dry. Part of her was scared. The other part seethed. "Are you sure she's not just trying to get a rise out of you? What's she upset about this time?"

"You. . .going out with Seth."

"Why?" The seething part took over.

"She says she found out something about him, but you won't answer her calls. She's furious."

"Did she say what it was?"

"No. But, April, this isn't about Seth. . .or you. I'm worried about your mother."

Rubbing her eyes, April nodded. "I'll call."

Why, just for once, couldn't it be about her? She closed the phone and sighed again, looking to Yvonne for sympathy.

"Trouble?"

"Probably just drama, but I guess I can't ignore it. I'm sorry."

"Take your time. I'll meet you at the study, and we can talk after." Yvonne gathered her purse and latte and waved good-bye.

April pressed 4 on her phone and waited. Her mother didn't bother with "Hello."

"Mom. . .settle down. I can't understand you."

"I just found out." The voice coming through April's phone rasped, as if she'd been yelling for hours. "I went to the library and searched the newspaper files."

"For Seth?" Seething might become a permanent state.

"I'm not going to lose another daughter to that man!"

April rolled her eyes. "And what did you find?"

"I'll tell you what I found. Seth Bachelor is married."

eleven

April clutched her Bible to her chest like a shield as she walked up to a stone house with no front yard. Next to the shiny red door with a brass kick plate, a burnished bronze plaque declared it to be on the Historic Registry of Homes. April touched the bottom of the antique door knocker but couldn't make herself use it.

She didn't want to be here. But not showing would have raised too many questions. If she could just shut out the picture and her mother's voice until she got home and had time to sort this through. Her brain felt as though she'd head butted an electric fence. After the jolt had come the fuzzy numbness that wouldn't allow her to formulate a concise thought, let alone a rational next step.

Confront him. That's what she needed to do. But when? And how? If she hadn't taken out a fraction of her agitation on gunning her engine and turning the radio up full blast, she might have done exactly what she wanted to do: march into this house and slap Seth Bachelor's square hypocritical jaw.

How was she going to sedate these emotions and act normal? How was she going to ignore the conversation that kept replaying in her brain?

The picture is right in front of me, April. I e-mailed you a copy.

Maybe he's divorced, Mom. Would that have made her feel any better?

Don't you think I thought of that? There's no record of a divorce.

What if his wife died? Why would he hide something like that?

April Jean, give me some credit for being a thinking human being. I checked the death records.

Still not convinced, she'd run home to check her e-mail before coming to the study. There was the picture. . .Seth in a long-tailed tuxedo, the new Mrs. Bachelor, née Brenda Cadwell, in a scoop-necked dress.

Seth is married. The words became a refrain to every thought. No wonder he'd seemed vague about why he was in Pine Bluff. He was hiding out. Did Mrs. Brenda Bachelor even know where he was? Or maybe they were still together, and he was living a double life. Were there children involved? In three years, they could have had two children. Was he sending child support?

It was all too easy to imagine two little children with Seth's dark hair and dimples. Two little girls, maybe, sitting at the kitchen table, waiting for food that didn't exist, finally rummaging in empty cupboards and a bare refrigerator until they found a half-empty package of stale soda crackers and the remains of a jar of grape jelly.

A car door slammed behind her, zapping her into the present. She tapped the brass knocker against the door.

&

They'd saved a seat for her, right between him and Yvonne on the extra long couch. Why hadn't she taken it? During introductions, her smile had made the rounds, landing on each person to Seth's right, hopping over him, and continuing with everyone to his left. He'd seen her talking to Yvonne before the study began, so she wasn't avoiding her. She was avoiding him.

Seth stared across the room at April, sitting cross-legged on the braided rug by the Franklin stove. Her rust-colored blouse brought out the reddish tones in her hair and reflected in spots of color on her cheeks. Not once in the fifteen minutes since she'd walked in had she made eye contact with him. What had he done now?

He sifted through what he remembered of the couple of times they'd talked since their breakfast at Sunrise and couldn't come up with anything she might have misconstrued. Had he inadvertently said something to make her mad? Was she simply losing interest? Had she really ever been interested? Why did women have to be so multifaceted? Just when you think you're getting to know one of them, a whole other side pops up that you didn't know existed. He forced his focus back on Pastor Owen, who was asking them to turn to the thirteenth chapter of Second Corinthians while he read aloud.

"'Examine yourselves to see whether you are in the faith; test yourselves. Do you not realize that Christ Jesus is in you—unless, of course, you fail the test?'"

A test. That's what he needed. An MMPI for every woman he met. *Hi, I'm Seth Bachelor. Glad to meet you. I'd like you to take the Minnesota Multiphasic Personality Inventory before a single word comes out of your mouth.*

That's the only way he'd be sure of finding someone who really was what she appeared to be. He'd let himself believe that April Douglas wasn't like so many of the women he'd met. She was a straight shooter, not a game player. If she didn't like something, she said so. So what statement was she making by sitting across the room and avoiding eye contact? He'd never been good at reading signals. He needed words. And he'd drag them out of her as soon as the study was over.

Things between them had been precarious right from the start. So what was it about her that made him keep coming back? She was good at letting him talk about himself, asking just the right questions at the right times. But that could be nothing more than her reporter training. She was funny, in the subtle kind of way he loved. Her compassion for others was genuine. He'd seen nothing in her that he'd label egotistical or vain. That alone was worth a ton of points.

He'd felt a bit off balance since the moment they'd met. . .and it wasn't all that bad a feeling. The sudden realization surprised him. In the past, he'd hated unpredictable relationships. The last few weeks had felt a lot like tracking an F5 tornado.

And he was loving it.

Looking down at his open Bible, he willed his mind to stay on task. Pastor Owen was reading verse eleven.

" 'Finally, brothers, good-by. Aim for perfection, listen to my appeal, be of one mind, live in peace. And the God of love and peace will be with you. Greet one another with a holy kiss.' "

A holy kiss. . .it had crossed his mind more than once in the past few days. Apparently he wouldn't be obeying that command any time soon.

He studied her, the way she toyed with the tassel on her bookmark, the uncomfortable-looking straightness of her posture. She'd glued her attention on Pastor Owen and his wife Audrey, appearing to be soaking in every word they uttered. Looking closer, he could tell that her glazed eyes weren't focused. Clearly, her mind wasn't on Second Corinthians.

At least they had that in common.

❧

There was a reason why April had participated in forensics rather than drama in high school. She could give an extemporaneous speech that would make a vegetarian order prime rib, but she was lousy at pretending to be someone else. Her broadcast classes had taught her to tuck her emotions into the cubbyholes of her psyche, but apparently that only worked in front of a camera or a microphone. Her training wasn't coming through for her now.

She realized too late that sitting across the room from Seth was a huge mistake. The thought of sitting close enough to smell his aftershave and feel his body heat had made her woozy. She'd opted for a spot on the floor, but now she was in his line of vision. Though she managed not to look directly at him, her peripheral scanning kept tabs on him. She was pretty sure his eyes hadn't left her face for an entire hour.

So she'd been right to distrust him in the beginning. No wonder the man had anger issues. Sure, there had been teases of the kind of man she'd always dreamed of—attentive, understanding, patient, creative—but none of that mattered now. Unless. . .what if he hadn't really deceived her? What if his wife had died in a different state? Her death certificate wouldn't be filed in Minnesota then, would it? Would the same be true of divorce records? Or what if, even now, Brenda Bachelor lay in a permanent coma, brain-dead from an accident? Maybe an accident that was Seth's fault?

But he would have told her something like that. Or Yvonne would have told her. It's not the kind of thing he'd hide from his church friends, his support system.

No imagined scenario gave him an easy out. The man had been—apparently still was—married.

At least she'd found out the truth before any real feelings for him had taken root. As it was, she might lose a night's sleep, but she refused to lose any tears.

Her neck and shoulders ached from sitting in the same rigid position. She had to move, but it had to be calculated. When her gaze left the front of the room, she couldn't let it sweep across Seth. She leaned back against the freestanding fireplace and turned her head to the left, away from Seth. At that angle, she was staring directly at Trace and Sydney McKay, newlyweds who somehow managed to hold hands while flipping through their respective Bibles.

As director of the chamber of commerce, Sydney collected rent checks from Yvonne and April every month. Over the course of a year, April had gotten to know her well. Just weeks after Caitlyn died, Sydney had announced her engagement. Though they were at very different seasons in their lives, they'd formed a bond, following the apostle Paul's words: "Rejoice with those who rejoice; mourn with those who mourn." April thought back to Trace and Sydney's wedding. Candlelight, a flowing dress encrusted with crystals, pale peach orchids, a wedding cake covered in chocolate and lacy white icing. And the groom, waiting at the altar with misty eyes. . .

April blinked, shocked by the sting of tears.

She looked down at her open Bible and forced herself to read and reread chapter thirteen of Second Corinthians. Verse eight jumped out at her. "For we cannot do anything against the truth, but only for the truth." *Lord, grant me the strength to speak the truth.*

Lost in outlining the speech that would corner Seth into the truth, April was startled by the sound of her name. Yvonne was talking about her.

". . .Remember that we prayed for her after her sister died, and I'm sure a lot of you have heard her radio program, *Slice of Life*, on Saturday afternoons. She's fulfilling a list that she made with her sister, experiences that celebrate life, I guess you'd say, and she's sharing her adventures with her listeners. Anyway, she's organizing a day hike on the Superior Trail for a week from Sunday. Anybody here interested in going?"

Heat flooded April's face. *Not now, Yvonne.* This time, her training came to her rescue, and she smiled and nodded like the cool, calm professional she didn't feel like. "I'm thinking of doing a five-mile loop, starting at Gooseberry Falls. It'll be a slow pace, so even if you're not an experienced hiker, it shouldn't be difficult. If you're interested, just e-mail Yvonne, and I'll get in contact with you." *Now shift the focus to someone else, please.*

"Let's see a show of hands. Who thinks they'd like to go?" Yvonne looked around the room as she asked.

Yvonne's hand lifted slowly, tentatively in reply to her own question, prompting April's mouth to open spontaneously. "You're going?"

Yvonne almost pulled off the look of offense. "I like the outdoors." The circle burst into laughter. Obviously, they knew her well. "So who's going to join us?"

Five hands rose. One of them was Seth's.

Trying her hardest to concentrate on the closing prayer, April found it impossible. Her mind painted pictures of what could have been. . .climbing the rise to Gooseberry Falls, her hand in Seth's, picking their way across the river on lichen-covered rocks, falling into his arms when her foot slipped. . . . The prayer ended, and the room buzzed with a dozen conversations at once. April stood, frantically searching for someone to talk to while she regrouped her resolve. But it was too late. She'd barely gotten to her feet when Seth crossed the room and stopped a foot in front of her. "Can we go outside for a minute?"

This wasn't the way she wanted the scene to play. She'd planned on being the one to say, "We need to talk." She'd planned on being in control. Setting her Bible on an end table, she nodded.

❧

"What's wrong, April?" He leaned against the seat of a pale blue and shiny black motorcycle, legs crossed at the ankles, arms folded over his chest, tightening the sleeves of his dark blue T-shirt. He scanned her face, patient once again.

What happened to the fury that she needed to carry this through? Why did her spine turn to Jell-O around this man? She took a deep breath and blew it out, puffing wind into her own sails.

"I think I should be asking what's wrong with you. What's wrong with a guy who's living a lie—or a double life?"

"What in the world are you talking about?"

"Isn't there some little detail you failed to tell me before you asked me out?"

Seth's brow creased. "April, I'm sorry. I have no clue what

you're getting at. Spell it out."

Her hands clamped on her hips. "My mother found your wedding announcement."

He stared at her, but she wasn't falling for the blank look. He wasn't even going to defend himself or try lying his way out? Her indignation returned with a vengeance. "Let me jog your memory. You get married, you take a picture, you put it in the paper. . . ." Her voice amplified with each word, but she didn't care. The tears she'd vowed not to shed teetered on her lashes.

Of all the expressions she would have expected from him, a smile was not one of them. Slowly it spread, deepening his dimple, forming little river deltas next to his eyes. April felt heat creep from her solar plexus to her temples. Could blood actually boil?

His hand reached for her shoulder. She jerked away. The infuriating smile didn't fade.

"But sometimes, if your fiancée's best friend works for a newspaper, you pose for the picture, you put it in the paper. . . and you *don't* get married."

twelve

Check your facts; know your sources. The line had been drummed into her in school. She knew it like she knew her own name. Why in the world had she chosen this particular time to listen to her mother? She should have checked the public records. But the picture was evidence. It hadn't crossed her mind to question it. Who took wedding pictures before a wedding?

April's eyes opened, her jaw locked tight. Beneath the pineapple-shaped globe of a streetlamp, the blue on the Harley glowed like Caribbean water. Seth's eyes appeared more black than brown—polished ebony, fixed on hers, holding her captive.

"You. . .didn't. . .get married?"

He shook his head. His eyes danced. "Still Bachelor."

He was playing with her, relishing her humiliation, yet the message that came through his teasing smile was unexpected. Grace. He wasn't mad. She'd cornered him like a deranged banshee, but he wasn't mad.

"I came frighteningly close to marrying the wrong woman, but I didn't."

The tears rolled over their banks, topping humiliation with fresh embarrassment. "I'm sorry." She fished a tissue out of her pocket.

Seth stood and took a step toward her. "You and I are getting to be experts at new beginnings, aren't we?"

All she could do was nod.

"Are you up for a moonlight ride?"

Wiping her nose, she nodded again, still fixed on the midnight glint in his eyes. A smile finally unparalyzed her face. "Promise you won't get all astronomical on me?"

"Five minutes of moon phases, max. Maybe ten on Mercury. If we stay up late enough, we'll be able to see it in the north-western sky." He grinned, turned, and unlatched the trunk compartment, pulling out a half helmet, two black leather jackets, and two pairs of gloves. His own helmet hung from a silver hook beneath the trunk. "Pays to keep a spare." He held out the helmet, but when she grabbed it, he didn't let go. "Before the thought hits your pretty head, this did not belong to my ex-fiancée."

"Thank you." His reassurance hadn't come before the thought, but it did put it to rest.

April walked around to the opposite side of the bike as she zipped the jacket and fastened the strap on the helmet. "I love this color."

"Suede Blue Pearl."

"Anniversary edition, huh?" She ran her hand across the curve of the gas tank.

Seth stopped, one hand partway into a leather glove. "You do know something about Harleys."

April glanced down at the Harley logo, silver wings up-turned against an orange and black background. Above the wings was printed 105 YEARS; below them, it said, "1903–2008."

"Yep, I know my bikes."

"I'm impressed." Seth tucked his sleeves into his gauntlet gloves. "Ready?"

"All set."

He turned and reached out for the left grip. His hand stopped in midair. Turning, he grinned at her then touched his gloved fingertips to the anniversary logo. "I really, really hate being gullible. It'll be a wilder ride because of that, you know." He swung his leg over the seat.

April stepped onto the foot pad. Holding onto Seth's shoulder, she hopped on. As he revved the motor, she yelled in his ear. "Bring it on!"

Seth did a U-turn and headed north, out of town. The air that had felt balmy when they'd walked outside now chilled April's cheeks. She wrapped her arms a little tighter around Seth's chest. When the speed limit changed to fifty-five, she felt the gears change. The vibration increased, the motor roared. The road curved as they climbed the bluff. Molding her body to his, she leaned into the turn with him. They flew over the crest of a rise. April's breath caught, and she felt like she'd left her stomach at the top of the hill. The wind rushed, and her eyes watered as they whipped along a straightaway and began to ascend again. Her hair slapped against the jacket collar. The road dipped, and they hit a pocket of cold air. April ducked closer into Seth's shoulders to block the wind.

Yvonne's words came to mind. *Experiences that celebrate life.* This moment, maybe her first in well over a year, was a celebration.

Seth had asked her if she could stand ten hours on a Harley.

Absolutely.

❧

"I was engaged to the second runner-up in the Miss St. Cloud Pageant."

"Brenda Cadwell."

"Mm-hm."

They sat on an orange blanket embroidered with Harley-Davidson emblems. Below them, the lights of Pine Bluff scattered like diamonds across the valley.

"Very prestigious." April watched his reaction, wondering how the breakup had really affected him.

"Yeah, that's what I thought when I first met her. She was a broadcasting student, shadowing the manager of the station I worked at for a class she was taking. I knew who she was before she introduced herself. I'd seen some of the pageant coverage. I was blown away when she asked me out."

"*She* asked *you?*"

A wry smile pulled at his mouth. "Yeah. Should have seen the manipulation red flags, but I was so caught up in the fact that she'd chosen little ol' me. I was blind right up until a week before the wedding."

"What happened?"

Seth picked up a stone and tossed it over the side of the bluff. It pinged against the rocks, the sound trailing off in the dark abyss. "I got a clue from her sister that there were a few little things she'd failed to mention in the two years we'd dated. Like the fact that she'd maxed out two credit cards and then run up thirty thousand dollars on Daddy's accounts, which she'd promised to pay back. All told, we would have started our marriage sixty-four thousand dollars in debt."

A long, low whistle slipped through April's lips. "All for the wedding?"

"No. Her parents and I covered the wedding bills as they came along. She'd charged clothes, jewelry, makeup, spa services. . .anything to decorate herself. And she'd hidden the debt from me." He pitched another rock. "When I confronted her, she denied it. The debt was one thing. The sin of omission and then the lying was what I couldn't get past. I could only guess at what else she'd forgotten to mention."

"So you broke it off a week before the wedding?"

"Worse than that. I did a credit check on her, and when she denied everything, I wanted to believe her. So I did some research. It took a few days to double-check everything. There was no mistake. I broke up with her an hour before the rehearsal dinner."

"Whoa. I'm picturing a rather angry bride."

Smile lines bracketed Seth's mouth. "I think 'livid' is the correct word. She drew blood when she launched the ring at me."

"Ouch."

"A couple weeks before the wedding, she insisted on having wedding pictures of the two of us taken at a studio. Had to have the right lighting, you know." He shook his head. "Her roommate worked for the paper and sidestepped the usual policy for her, letting her submit a picture early so it would come out in the Sunday morning paper. By the time they thought of it, the paper had already gone to press."

April studied the relaxed set of his jaw. She'd seen him upset enough to know that his jaw muscles usually bulged when he was angry. "You seem to have dealt pretty well with it. I think I'd still be bitter."

"That was the amazing thing. The second I told her I wasn't going to marry her—in front of her parents, by the way—the relief was unbelievable."

"But you weren't miserable with her before that?"

Seth shrugged. "Did you ever have a tag on the neck of a shirt that was stiff and scratchy, and all day long, you're kind of subconsciously aware of it, but you're too busy to focus on it? That's what our relationship was like. On some level, it wasn't feeling right. She wasn't interested in much of anything I like to do. I sometimes wonder if she was interested in me at all, or if she was just addicted to the male attention and any guy would do. Honestly, I think she would have been just as happy dating a full-length mirror."

It was April's turn to pick up a smooth, flat rock and pitch it into the darkness. "I'm glad you found out before it was too late. Do you still have contact with her?"

Seth's sigh carried notes of weariness mingled with frustration. "Only when I have to. Unfortunately, our paths cross often. . .professionally."

"I'm sorry I lashed out at you. I should have checked the facts."

"Forget it. A wedding announcement sure looks like fact. Besides. . ." His fingertip traced the outline of her hand on the blanket. "Your righteous wrath was kind of flattering."

April aimed her smile at the distant lights. "And why is that?"

"Because it just might mean that in spite of all our ups and downs, you're developing some feelings for me."

"And you'd consider that a good thing?"

His arm slid around her shoulders. "I'd consider that a very good thing."

☙

He'd been waiting for the right moment to put his arm around her. When he did, she nestled against his shoulder and looked up at him. Close enough to kiss. Slowly, he bent his head toward hers.

"I hear we're in for a storm tomorrow."

The sparkle in her eyes told him she knew full well what he'd been about to do. And he was pretty sure the distraction technique was more to lead him on than away. He'd gladly play that game, and he had just the strategy to make it a short round.

"Thunderstorms are usually instigated by several factors: sufficient moisture, usually at low levels near the surface; a vertical profile in the atmosphere that is unstable, meaning a parcel of air will continue to rise if given a push upward"—he gestured with his hand—"and a mechanism to give the air parcels a push, such as a cold or warm front. Simply stated, moisture, instability, and lift. When these three things come together within certain parameters, we can be pretty sure of a thunderstorm."

Her eyes stayed fixed on his, her bottom lip firmly clamped between her teeth. She wasn't going to cave in as easily as he'd thought.

"It is possible that thunderstorms can arise with just two of the three parameters. . .for example, when there is no surface front or other mechanism to lift the air, but there is great instability and plenty of moisture. If the air parcels rise"—he inched closer and lifted his hand to illustrate—"due to the instability and there is nothing to stop them, a shower or thunderstorm may—"

Her hand reached out and grabbed his in midair. "Okay. I surrender." Her head pressed into his shoulder. "Let's. . ." Her eyes closed. "Let's just. . .talk about tornadoes." Her eyes popped open, her lips spread into an amazing smile.

"O. . .kay. . ."

Her fingertip pressed against his lips, sending prickly sensations down his spine. "Specifically, when do we get to chase one?"

Seth laughed against her finger and then graced it with a featherlight kiss. She lowered her hand but rested it, palm up, on her knee. Saving his kiss? "You do realize, my dear, that there has to be a tornado in the vicinity in order to chase it."

An elbow boxed his right side. "And here I thought you'd create one just for me."

"I would if I could." Her deep blue eyes suddenly seemed a bit too deep, a little too inviting. Folding his legs under him, he turned sideways to face her. "June is the biggest month for tornadoes in Minnesota, so we should have an opportunity soon. I'll introduce you to Darren, the storm-chasing guru. Are you free Friday night?"

"Yes."

"Darren's coming over for pizza. How about if I ask him to bring his family, and we'll make it a five-and-a-half-some."

Her eyes narrowed. "Ah. One child and one on the way?"

He nodded. "Denisha is due in about a month. Wesley is four. . .going on fifty."

"Wesley. . .nice name. Thank goodness they didn't pick a *D* name."

"I tried to convince them to give him my middle name. Darren, Denisha, and Dalton—has a nice ring, don't you think?"

"Your middle name is Dalton?" Amusement danced in her eyes before she discreetly looked over his shoulder.

"Yeah. . .I don't like it either. I was named for my dad's alma mater in Georgia."

"How. . .significant."

"Just laugh and get it over with."

She did.

"Okay, that's enough. You must be blessed with a very normal middle name."

Once again, she laughed. "It's Jean, and I hate it. It would be perfect if I'd wanted to be a country music star."

"April Jean will be singin' for us t'nite, folks," he twanged.

"Anyway, about the tornado guru. . ."

"Hey, that was a meaningful rabbit trail. We learned something about each other."

"If you ever say my name through your nose like that again, I'll use your middle name on the air the next time you call my show."

"Yes ma'am." He loved how easily she made him laugh and lose track of what he was saying. "Friday night. . .Darren will cure your fear of tornadoes. There's nothing he loves more than showing spine-chilling videos of his close calls."

"And that will cure me?"

"You'll have chase fever before the end of the night. You'll be begging for the chance to see an F4 up close and personal."

"Right." She stretched her lips in a pretend smile.

He looked down at her hand, pressed against the blanket, and touched the silver ring on her index finger, sliding it back and forth. "I don't know if I've actually put it into words yet, but I admire your courage."

"I'm anything but courageous." She crossed her legs to mirror him, and they sat knee to knee.

"Do you know what Mark Twain said?"

"No. What did Mark Twain say?" Even in the engulfing

darkness, he could see the gleam in her eyes.

"That courage is not the absence of fear but resistance to the mastery of fear. He said, 'Except a creature be part coward, it is not a compliment to say it is brave.'"

"Well then, I guess I qualify. I felt like the lion in *The Wizard of Oz* at the top of the water tower."

"But the point is. . .you were at the top of the water tower." Seth raised his right hand, sinking his fingers into her hair. He felt her take a tremulous breath. As he leaned toward her, he lifted her chin with his other hand. Millimeters from her lips, he whispered, "I think you're very brave."

Her eyes closed; her lips parted.

And Seth pointed. "Look, a meteor."

April's eyes jarred open and then followed the line of his arm to the white trail disappearing into the invisible horizon. She smiled, shook her head just the tiniest bit. "Can't you just call it a falling star?"

"But it really isn't a star at all." He matched her knowing smile. "The streak of light is caused by tiny bits of dust and rock falling into the atmosphere and burn—"

Her fingers sealed his lips, slowly pulled away. Her eyes closed again.

And he kissed her.

thirteen

"You're listening to Christian R&B on this super sunny Thursday afternoon in beautiful downtown Pine Bluff. This is April Douglas. We just heard a Glenn Kaiser song, "In the Ocean of His Love," a personal favorite of mine. Love those acoustic rhythms. Drowning in the ocean of His love. . .that's where we all need to be, isn't it?"

Words gushed like the St. Croix after a spring rain, in spite of a night full of daydreams in which sleep eluded her. April was in her zone, incredulous, as always, that someone was willing to pay her a salary, be it ever so meager, for doing what she loved. She looked up at Jill and grinned, getting the now familiar thumb in the air in response.

"We're taking a little break from routine in a minute. I'm going to give a little teaser of my show, *Slice of Life*, that's now airing live from three to five thirty every Saturday. I'll take as many calls as we can fit into a five-minute slot. Here's your assignment: In one word, describe how you're feeling today, positive or negative. No holds barred, just keep it family friendly. After that, give me a single sentence to explain why you chose that word. So break out the thesaurus, and let's see how creative we can get. I'll start taking your calls in forty seconds." She pushed the button that played a public service announcement for the local food bank.

Her monitor began filling with names before the break was over. She watched the clock, counting down to the green light, and leaned into her microphone. "You're listening to KPOG, praising our God in Minnesota. My screen is lit with Pine Bluffians ready to share the single word that best describes how they're feeling today. Shane, what's your word?"

"Grateful."

April gave an inward sigh. This was exactly what she'd been afraid of—and the reason she was keeping this experiment to five minutes. An hour of Christianese—*grateful, blessed, happy, thankful. . .*—would be more than she could handle. She'd been hoping for some more nitty-gritty words. "And why did you choose 'grateful,' Shane?"

"Because today is my eighteenth birthday, and thanks to some really forgiving people, I'm having pizza with my youth group tonight instead of celebrating all alone in a jail cell."

Okay, so she'd been wrong. Goose bumps dotted her arms. "Our God is awesome, isn't He?" She swallowed, clearing the roughness the unexpected emotion had brought. "Happy Birthday, Shane. I hope your day is incredible. If you'd be willing to share your story sometime, leave your number with Orlando."

She scanned the list, not the least bit surprised to see Seth in the queue. Was this going to be a regular occurrence? She smiled at her reflection on the monitor. Her listeners would start suspecting something if she took his calls every week. "Melissa, what's your word?"

"Harebrained."

So it wasn't going to be a predictable few minutes after all. "Can't wait to hear your reason, Melissa."

"I've been searching high and low for my dish detergent. My son just found it—right behind the catsup in the fridge."

Five more calls produced five more surprises. Apparently her listeners had taken the thesaurus suggestion seriously. *Magnanimous, exasperated, worshipful, goofy,* and *whimsical. . .* she really could fill an hour like this.

"Now, on to our final caller. Seth, what one word describes you today?" She closed her eyes.

"Breathless. Because I saw a falling star last night and haven't been able to catch my breath ever since."

❧

"You did what?" Her mother's voice, high and shrill, made the hair on the back of April's neck bristle.

April scrunched her face at Splash and Willy and turned the volume down on her phone. "You heard me, Mom. I went for a motorcycle ride with Seth."

"But. . ."

"He never got married. They took the picture before the wedding and then called it off."

"And you believe that?"

April rubbed a tight spot on her shoulder. "Yes."

"Baby. . ." It was a term her mother used like a weapon. "I don't have a good feeling about this. Take it from somebody who's been kicked around. . .this man is only going to use you."

"You don't know the first thing about him! All you know is that he's a man. There are good men out there, Mom."

A low huff came through the earpiece. "This is moving way too fast."

"What is? We went out a couple times and watched the sunrise together." *And kissed.* She picked up Snow Bear and twirled between the coffee table and the kitchen counter. This wasn't news her mother was going to hear.

Silence filled the next few seconds. She heard a slow exhale on the other end.

"Why did they call off the wedding?"

"It wasn't his fault, if that's what you mean. Let's talk about something else, okay? Midge said she's hoping you'll join her and Laura and Sue for lunch one of these days."

"Those church ladies don't want to hang out with me. They're just doing their Christian duty. I can't stomach pity."

April stared at Willy and Splash, stuck in their eternal battle-ready positions, and swallowed back the acerbic remarks that burned her throat. Never in her life had she met anyone as adept at eliciting pity as her mother. "I thought you liked Sue and Laura. If you give them a chance, I'm sure—"

A hollow sigh echoed through the phone. "Don't try to distract me, April. Believe me, I understand that you want a man in your life, but you can't just jump at the first guy who talks sweet to you."

"A gentle answer turns away wrath. Do not repay anyone evil for evil. If it is possible, as far as it depends on you, live at peace with everyone." She repeated every peacekeeping verse she knew, but her blood still pounded in her temples. *Lord, I don't think it's possible to live at peace with her.* "He's not a sweet-talker. He's just a nice, genuine guy."

"Sure he is. A nice, genuine guy who left your sister in the rain to get chilled to the bone and—"

"It didn't happen like that." April set Snow Bear on the couch and slumped down beside him. She massaged the spot between her eyes that throbbed with every breath. She'd decided not to bring it up, ever, but living at peace didn't always mean biting your tongue. She took a deep breath. "Why did you sign the permission slip for her to go with the storm chasers?"

Silence. A muffled gasp. "I never. . ."

"They won't take minors storm tracking without parental permission."

"But I. . .I don't remember. There were so many papers, insurance forms, medical reports. I don't. . .remember." A soft sob ended her words.

And guilt ended April's internal rage. Deep down, she hurt for her mother. Like simmering magma, that pain was at the center of her very being, sometimes erupting in sympathy, other times in avoidance. She understood pain; she understood betrayal and bitterness. What she couldn't accept was wallowing in it and sucking everyone else in with you.

"I'm sorry. I shouldn't have brought that up."

"So it was my fault." A chilling deadness shrouded her mother's voice.

"No. You gave Caitlyn a gift, just like Seth and his friend did. That was the best day she'd had in a long time."

"But it killed her."

"No, Mom. Leukemia killed her. It would have anyway; you know that."

Another long, quiet stretch spanned the seconds. April chose not to fill it, hoping her words would sink in.

"Thank you." The words were so soft that April wasn't sure she'd heard them.

"I love you, Mom." Not easy to say but true nonetheless.

"I. . .love you, too."

⋅⋆

Friday night came almost too quickly. Anticipation and anxiety vied for center stage as April's maroon Grand Prix rolled to a stop in front of Seth's house. It wasn't at all what she'd expected.

She'd pictured him in one of the newer, more secluded homes on the bluff. A home built for efficiency, with clean lines, neutral colors, and minimalist decorating. That would fit him. Instead, she found herself on Minnetonka Street, just three blocks off Main, in front of a small, two-story symmetrical white house with black shutters, probably built in the thirties. Dormer windows jutted heavenward like raised eyebrows, giving the house a welcoming, smiley face appeal. Two brass lights on either side of the door added dimples to the face—just like its owner's.

Seth Bachelor, you are a man of surprises. Grabbing her purse and the pan of brownies she'd baked before work, she got out of the car. As she walked up the steps from the sidewalk to the walkway that led to the house, she assessed her look. Brown wedge sandals peeked out from the hem of her jeans. She'd painted her toenails the exact shade of the two inches of coral tank top that showed beneath a brown T-shirt. She'd used hot rollers to add a bit more curl than usual and wore small turquoise and sterling earrings and a matching necklace. *Not too shabby.* It felt good to feel good.

For months, she hadn't really cared.

April stepped between the two sculpted evergreens, twice as tall as she was, that guarded the front door and rang the doorbell. Before the second chime, Seth opened the door. April held out the nine-by-thirteen-inch pan covered in aluminum foil. It gave her something to do in the first awkward seconds when she wondered if he'd kiss her.

He did. Leaning over the pan, his lips touched hers for only a moment, but his eyes loitered. "Wow." He stood back, giving her room to walk past him. "You look amazing."

"Thank you." She wasn't usually the blushing kind, but the capillaries under her skin couldn't seem to stay constricted under the heat of his gaze. Was it proper to tell a man that he also looked—and smelled—amazing? He wore flip-flops, jeans, and a formfitting black Harley T-shirt that appeared to have seen a lot of motorcycle rides. The shoulders were slightly sun-faded, the seams frayed, stirring thoughts of riding behind him without a helmet, hair dancing in the wind, her face resting against the worn-thin shirt. Which would bring her closer to the source of the musky aftershave and the dark stubble shadowing his square jaw line. "Should I put this in the kitchen?"

"Sure. I'll give you part of the tour on the way." He led her through an arched doorway into the living room. White walls, hardwood floors, black couch and loveseat with huge red accent pillows. Above an arched brick fireplace, also painted white, hung a framed black-and-white photograph of a seemingly endless flight of shadowy stone steps, lit by old gaslight streetlamps. In front of the fireplace, a shaggy white rug begged for bare feet.

"Wow." It was her turn to use the word.

Another arched doorway led to the dining room. The walls were bare, the round black table held a square white plate with a cluster of blue and white baseball-sized glass balls. Dishes in the same color, but a different pattern, lined the shelves of a black oriental-inspired china cabinet.

Seth swept his hand toward the doorway to the kitchen. If April's mouth had closed since she'd entered the living room, it would have dropped open again now.

Cupboards, countertop, appliances, and tiled floor, all hospital white, created a blank canvas for vibrant splashes of cobalt blue and lime green. An oversize handblown glass bowl in swirls of blue and white took up the middle of the table in a white-painted breakfast nook. A smaller bowl of the same color, filled with oranges, was the only object on the ceramic counter. Valances, striped blue and new-leaf green, hung over the nine-pane windows. Small pots of wheatgrass graced the sill above the sink.

She'd gotten the minimalist part right. The color was unexpected. And then a question mark poked its tail into her amazement. Had *she* done the decorating? Was this the touch of the almost-Mrs. Bachelor?

"Who did your decorating?" Her voice strained around the lump in her throat. Maybe he wouldn't notice.

Seth smiled. A smile that said he'd heard the question behind her question. He took the pan from her hands and set it on the counter, leaving nothing but air between them. His hands rested on her arms. "I did. Just me, all by myself. Alone. For me alone."

There was nothing she could do but laugh. "I'm really not that insecure." *Usually.*

"Remember what I said on the bluff?" His fingertips found the bottom of her chin. "A little insecurity is just as flattering as righteous wrath."

"I'll try to rememb—" Her words got lost in his lips.

His arms wrapped around her. Her hands reached up to his shoulders.

And the doorbell rang.

fourteen

"It's a college thing."

Denisha Williams rolled huge brown eyes toward the kitchen ceiling as Seth and Darren finished an elaborate and ridiculous high-five, low-five, under-duck-and-twirl hand-shake routine.

April shook her head. "Are they always this nuts together?"

"Always."

The two men contrasted like photograph negatives. Seth, in his black shirt with his arms barely tanned—Darren, his skin the color of strong coffee, wearing a white Harley shirt.

Leaning toward Denisha, April whispered, "I missed the memo about wearing Harley shirts."

Denisha's shoulder-length black curls swayed when she laughed. She rested both hands on the red blouse stretched over her extended belly. "It's eerie how often they dress alike. I'm convinced they're twins separated at birth." Her dark eyes sparkled as she laughed.

Light, running footsteps and a tumult of claws echoed from the hardwood floor in the living room. "Se. . .*th*." Wesley bounded into the kitchen, followed by Maynard, the grizzly bear Seth tried passing off as a dog. Both skidded to a stop in front of Seth.

"Make me fly, Se*th*."

"He's working on his *t–h* sounds," Denisha whispered.

Seth ruffled Wesley's thick black curls and picked him up by the back of his coveralls. "This plane's gonna be too heavy to get off the ground pretty soon."

Wesley made airplane sounds as Seth flew him around the

dining room table twice and back into the kitchen.

"I think the men should make a quick trip upstairs to see my new telescope until the good little women call us for pizza. Right, Wes?" Seth winked in April's direction.

Darren planted a kiss on top of Denisha's head. "We'll do dishes."

As the men walked out of the kitchen, Denisha squeezed April's arm. "I'm glad we're getting a little girl time." She pointed toward the breakfast nook. "I gotta get off my feet." The bench creaked as she sat down, with no room to spare between her stomach and the table. "It's so good to finally meet you. I suppose it's cliché to say I've heard so much about you, but it's true." She leaned her forearms on the table. "I'm so sorry about your sister. Darren was devastated when he heard about it."

"Seth and your husband blessed her with a wonderful day."

"Thank you. That's very gracious."

"So what have you heard about me?"

"It's all good." Denisha glanced toward the stove. "Okay, the oven timer's going off in seven minutes, so I'm just gonna plunge right in. Are things getting serious between you two?"

April blinked. She hadn't expected an interrogation.

A ladylike snort answered April's awkward silence. "I can see it on your face." She folded her hands. "Seth is special to me. He dragged my husband back to the Lord a few years ago and saved our marriage. So I'm pretty protective of him. You know he's been hurt in the past, and all I'm asking is that you promise me you'll be honest with him—about everything."

It wasn't something she needed to think about. April rested her fingertips on Denisha's bangle bracelet. "You have my word on that."

❧

Wesley stood at eye level to the kitchen counter. "Can we watch tornado movies and eat in Man Room?"

April looked from Wesley to Denisha. "Man Room?"

"You'll see. If we're very, very good they'll take down the No Girls Allowed sign." Denisha handed a pizza pan to Darren and one to Seth and picked up a bowl of potato chips. "May we enter the inner sanctum?"

As if they'd practiced their routine, the men bowed simultaneously, ushering the way into the den with the hands that held the pizzas.

"You're right, it's eerie." April picked up paper plates and napkins and nodded to Denisha. "I'll follow you."

The hush in the dimly lit room was the first thing she noticed. As her eyes adjusted to the low light, she understood. Sound-absorbing plush black carpeting covered the floor, three walls, and the ceiling. Massive speakers and a flat-screen TV took up the fourth wall. Six recliners formed a curved row in front of a glass-topped coffee table that appeared to be at least five feet long.

Seth set the pizza on the table and opened a small black refrigerator. "Everybody help yourself to soda or water." He walked over to April. His fingers rested on hers before he took the plates from her. "Welcome to Man Room."

"It's an honor to be allowed in."

"Sit there." He pointed to the second recliner from the left end. "I'll hold your hand during the scary parts."

"The scary parts are the coolest!" Wesley grabbed Seth's forearm and hung like a little monkey. Turning to April, he said, "I chaseded a tornado today."

"You did?"

Seth raised his eyebrow and shook his head, and April bent down to Wesley's eye level. "What did it look like?"

"It was huuuuge and black, and it chomped houses like a T. rex, and I went right up next to it, and I wasn't scared even a bit."

"Well, maybe you can teach me to not be scared of tornadoes."

"Nah. I don't think so. 'Cause you're a girl like Mom and

girls are s'posed to be scared of T. rexes and tornadoes. But when you watch my dad's movies, you just gotta keep saying 'It's only a movie. It's only a movie.' 'Cause even though it used to be real, it's not like it's outside right now. 'Kay?"

&

"It's only a movie. It's only a movie." Seth whispered so close to her ear that his lips felt the cool smoothness of her silver and turquoise earrings. She'd been like a coiled spring for the past half hour.

Her eyes were riveted to the jostling footage that had been filmed through the windshield of Darren's van. A gray funnel swirled out of a black cloud and split into twin sisters. On the ground, lights flashed as the tornadoes flattened power lines and transformers. Darren's voice on the video shouted over the locomotive roar in the background. "I'm guessing wind speeds upwards of two hundred. An F3 for sure, maybe a 4. This storm is violent. Look at the action on either side. It's gonna do some damage if it doesn't change course. There's a subdivision just east of here. Let's hope the local weather guys got it right this time and gave them plenty of warning."

Seth tossed a crumpled napkin over April and Denisha, hitting Darren square on the head.

"Nothing personal, man." Darren's laugh said otherwise.

The scene changed to a different storm. This time, the sky was gunmetal gray, the supercell storm cloud white against the darkness. A shaft of lightning shot out of the cloud. Seth leaned forward, his pulse double-timing. This was footage he'd never seen. "Should be a funnel forming any minute," he said under his breath. Seconds later, a white snake dropped out of the cloud, sucking up trees like a vacuum hose. A barn, directly in its path, suddenly exploded. April jumped. Boards shot up into the cloud.

"Big tornado on the ground! I'm setting up the tripod!" Darren's voice yelled above the noise.

"Multivortex!" a second voice shouted. "You gettin' this on tape, Darren?"

"I got it. How many? I see three satellites."

"Four. One's pulling away. It's heading straight for us. Get in the car! Get in the car!"

The picture bounced. . .voices clamored. . .a shot of the inside of the car door. . .doors slammed. The car did a U-turn, and the camera panned to the rear window. "We can't outrun it! Let's try for the overpass!" A white funnel bore down on the speeding car. . .and the image froze on the screen.

Darren held a remote control in each hand. With his left hand, he slowly turned up the rheostat for the overhead LED track lights. "Thought April might need a break."

Wesley clapped.

April collapsed against the back of her seat. "You can't stop it there! What happened?"

"We made it to the overpass, which isn't really the smartest thing to do. I managed to loop one of the straps on my back-pack over a piece of rebar. The guy who was driving wasn't so lucky. He got sucked out and got hit with a chunk of debris. Had to have a dozen stitches."

"Awesome." Seth didn't even realize what he'd said until he caught April's eyes drilling into him. "I mean. . .sure glad he wasn't hurt worse."

Denisha patted April's hand. "You'll get used to it."

The look on April's face clearly said she wasn't sure she wanted to get used to it.

Darren threw the wadded napkin back at Seth. "She won't need to get used to it unless Weather Guy leaves the station in somebody else's hands and starts doing what he really wants to do."

Seth felt his jaw tighten involuntarily. "Drop it."

"I haven't brought it up for months." Darren leaned around the women and pointed a remote at him. "I could still line up back-to-back tours all the way through July." He shifted his position to include April in his pleading gaze. "What we'd do is set up week-long tours for people. We'd take a caravan of three or four vehicles up and down Tornado Alley, from North Dakota to the Rio Grande. And this is an awesome year for storms, perfect for launching our business." His voice lowered as his hand came to rest on Denisha's belly. "But I can't be gone that long this season. I need a partner."

"I'm sure you can find one." Seth's body language was as tense as his voice.

"I want you. Get yourself a decent manager so the station can get along without you for a week at a time. You'd be reachable 24-7. And your puny little town doesn't need a live weather forecast. Give them daily feed from the National Weather Service. They'll get over missing your handsome face."

"Not interested."

"Liar."

"Give it up, Darren. You're boring the ladies."

Darren locked brown eyes on April. "I've heard your radio show. That dream list your sister made. . .you're all about living life to the fullest, right? Don't you think that if people can afford it they should spend their lives doing what they love to do? Can't you talk some sense into this guy?"

"What does—"

"I *can't* afford it." Tension knotted Seth's gut. This wasn't a conversation he wanted to have again, especially not in front of April.

"You could if you'd quit pay—"

"I said, drop it!"

❧

Sandals and empty cake pan in one hand, a list of storm-watcher gear in the other, April padded up the stairs, avoiding the two steps that creaked the loudest. Laughter and music drifted down to meet her. Good. Yvonne had company. She wouldn't have to worry about being chatty tonight. What she needed was a hot bath and a good book. Definitely not a romance.

A third sound joined in as she reached the top step. A vacuum cleaner. Strange thing to be doing when you have visitors.

But the sounds weren't coming from Yvonne's apartment. They were coming from hers. Cautiously, she opened the door.

"Ahh!" Midge jumped, eyes popping like a Pekinese, and shut off the vacuum cleaner. "I didn't think you'd be home so early."

Yvonne, standing on the couch, waved at her with a feather duster, sending dust bits raining onto Snow Bear. "How was dinner?"

"What are you two doing?"

"Cleaning." They answered in unison.

"I see that. Why?" It wasn't like she kept the place a mess.

Midge plopped down in the rocker. "I'm keeping my promise. You went out with Seth, so I'm cleaning your apartment."

"And I'm trying to make up for not telling you the truth about him taking you to *Riverdance*." Yvonne hopped down. "Even though it all worked out for the best."

Maybe.

"So. . .do you like Seth's friends?" Midge asked at the same time Yvonne said, "Do you want to chase a tornado?"

I want to take a bath. She dropped her shoes at the door and took the cake pan into the kitchen. Leaning heavily on the counter that divided the two rooms, she gave a halfhearted smile. "You didn't have to do this, but thank you. The place hasn't been this clean in forever."

Midge whisked away her thanks. "You're welcome, but you're not answering the questions."

"Dinner was good, the people are nice, and I kind of get the storm-chasing adventure thing."

"But. . . ?" Yvonne sat down next to Snow Bear.

"But what?"

"Something didn't go right. I can tell."

Unfastening her necklace, April walked around the counter and sank into the other end of the couch. "I think I finally figured it out. I just don't get men." She picked a fleck of lint off Snow Bear's ear. "Think about it. . .how could I? No brothers, no grandfathers or uncles, a father who was more out of my life than in it. Guys are. . .they're not like us."

Her audience of two erupted in laughter. Midge, who'd been—at least outwardly—happily married for twenty-five years, was the first to regain her composure. "No truer words were ever spoken."

April tucked her feet beneath her. "Tonight—we're in the middle of watching storm footage—when Seth and his friend Darren get into this argument. Not a quiet one. I was ready to hightail it out of there when I looked over at Darren's wife. She's just sitting there munching on chips. Like she's watching a basketball game. But she knows these guys, so I stayed and watched; pretty soon their voices lowered, and in a couple minutes, they're talking about a sci-fi movie that's coming out next week. No 'I'm sorry.' It was like they both said what they had to say, and then it was over."

"Men are a lot like tornadoes."

"Midge! Did you just say something critical?"

Midge's shoulders rose to her ears. "God made tornadoes, too."

Yvonne nodded. "I've seen Kirk do that with his brothers a million times."

"It just scares me, knowing he's capable of yelling like that. When's he going to turn it on me?"

The rocking chair groaned as Midge bent forward, resting

her hand on April's knee. "Probably never. I know I've said it before, but don't make the mistake of putting your father's sins on every man you meet."

"I know. But why can't they just be more like us? Quieter and—"

"Cattier?"

"Midge! What's gotten into you?"

"Just speaking the truth. I think I'd rather take my chances with a man who lays it all out on the table than some of the women I've met who quietly stab you in the back."

"Me, too." Yvonne stood then stuck her hands in the pocket of her cardigan. "Oh, here—somebody called for you about an hour ago. She said it didn't matter how late you called her back."

April looked down at the scrap of paper. And a chill skittered down her back.

555-784-0938
Brenda Cadwell

fifteen

Water thundered over the stair-step rocks. The spray above Middle Gooseberry Falls split sunlight into a halo of color. Sitting next to Seth on a hardened lava flow below the falls, April skimmed her bare heels along the surface of the icy water then pulled her feet back to the sun-warmed rock.

"You're doing that like a girl." With both feet submerged, Seth talked through gritted teeth. "Just stick 'em in all at once." He gestured toward Yvonne's fiancé, Kirk, sitting beside him, feet also under water.

"And look as miserable as you two do just to prove I'm tough? No thanks."

Yvonne shook her platinum curls. "You guys have more pride in your little toes than we have in our whole bodies."

With a painful gasp, Kirk yanked his feet out of the water. A split second later, Seth copied his move. Both men writhed, accompanied by female laughter. Kirk reached out for Yvonne's hand. "I concede. You're a better man than I am, Seth. Come on, woman, help me walk some circulation into my legs."

As Seth lay back on his elbows, a look of triumph mixed with pain on his face, April rested her bare feet on his.

"Ah. . .heat. Thank you." He lifted his sunglasses. In the bright light, his eyes took on a bronze tinge.

The warmth soaking through the back of her North Face polo was now met by the heat sparked by those bronze eyes. Suddenly her feet on his seemed way too intimate. She shifted and copied his posture, resting back on her elbows. Nearer than she'd calculated. Not touching but close enough to smell that musky, earthy aftershave.

A herring gull scudded to a stop several yards away, lifted its head, and called into the air. Seth's little toe touched hers. "Perfect day," he whispered.

"Mm-hm."

It seemed the ideal setting to tell him the news that had been percolating in her head since Friday night. The news that had stolen her sleep and filled half a notebook with heady, adrenaline-driven ideas.

"You won't believe who called me the other night."

Seth rolled his fleece jacket into a ball and used it for a pillow, stretching out on the flat rock. "Who?" His voice sounded sleepy.

"Brenda."

Bolting to a sitting position, he whipped off his sunglasses. "Brenda. . .who?"

Your Brenda. No, he wouldn't find that amusing. "Brenda Cadwell."

"She called you? Why?" Suspicion dripped from his words.

April grinned. "To offer me a job."

❧

How could five little words turn a perfect day into a nightmare? He'd been lying there, more relaxed than he'd felt in months, stringing words together in his head—words that would describe his growing feelings for the woman with the honey blond hair who was so close to him he could smell the spicy, touch-of-vanilla scent of her.

And then she'd smacked him with a name that he was within weeks of never having to hear again.

She was effervescing before his eyes. Glowing like Sirius on a clear night. Her warm, lush radio voice painted the vision as detailed as an oil painting. A prime-time spot on a cable station three hours from Pine Bluff. She couldn't tell him what station, what town. The details were all being worked out. Her own talk show. Huh. . .where had Brenda gotten *that* idea? A Christian show on a secular station. What were the chances? April asked.

Behind his back, Seth's fist clenched on the green-tinged rock. *Slim to none.* Whatever Brenda Cadwell had up her sleeve, it wasn't good.

"It'll be an hour-long show, five days a week, to start with." April's fingers knit her hands into a ball. "And I get to pick the guests. Pretty much carte blanche, it sounds like."

"Hm. Where'd she get the idea for the format?"

Confusion wrinkled her forehead. He wanted to kiss it away, wanted to kiss away the last five minutes.

"She got the idea from you."

She certainly did. "She told you that?"

"Yes. She said you told her that I'd always dreamed of being a television talk show host. To be honest, it made me mad at first. I shared that with you in confidence."

Seth opened his mouth to defend himself, but she held up her hand.

"But then I realized that you'd told her about it because she's got the right connections. She's somebody who could make my dream come true."

Her eyes held his for a long moment. "I know the distance is an issue, but I'd be back here every weekend."

"When would you start?" His voice was as flat as his mood.

"In two weeks."

"Kind of soon."

"Well, it wouldn't air for another six weeks or so. I'd start out just lining up guests and working on promotion."

"And they'd pay you for that part?"

Her hands separated. She rubbed her palms on her knees. "I. . .assume so."

"What's your starting salary?"

"She couldn't say yet, just promised I'd have no complaints."

Promised. Brenda's promise. . .now there was an oxymoron if he'd ever heard one. "When is your interview scheduled?"

She recoiled, just a fraction of an inch. "That was. . .my interview. . .on the phone."

"Oh. Don't you need to talk to a manager?"

"Brenda is. . .in charge of hiring."

"She is, huh?"

&

Yvonne walked over and pointed at her watch. "Time to move on."

April nodded. Keeping the group on schedule was supposed to be her job. She picked up a sock, grateful for a reprieve from Seth's cross-examination. What was wrong with the man? Of course, she wanted him to express some sadness, but he seemed far more angry than sad. He knew how much this meant to her, didn't he? His barrage of questions was insulting. Didn't he know her well enough to know that she'd check it out carefully before accepting? The KOEK Web site said they were actively working to expand their programming and give the station a fresh, new image. She was going to be part of that new image.

Turning away from him, she used her purple bandana to dry between her toes and then slipped on her white liner socks. She yanked at the shoestrings of her dusty gray Raichle boots. Too tight. After tying them right, she stuffed her jacket in her day pack. As she zipped the pocket shut, Seth's hand jutted into the space between her and her walking stick. He blocked the sun, but the look on his face would suffice for sunlight. "Let's enjoy the day, okay?"

"Okay." Like a trained puppy, she held her hand out to him. It was becoming easier and easier to let his offenses slide. Was that a good or a bad thing? With her hand in his, she couldn't decide.

The seven of them scrambled across slippery rocks, climbed the outcroppings above the falls, and ended back on the shaded trail. April took the lead, with Seth right behind her, singing "Happy Trails." He'd rallied, but his mood still wasn't where it had been before she'd brought up the job offer. A few weeks ago, her response to his negativity would have been a cold shoulder, but she was learning to put a leash on her emotions, to let things play out. The more it sank in that the males of the species processed conflict in a whole different way, the more she was willing to think before she acted. And little by little, she was beginning to accept that not all—probably not most—men had hair triggers like her father.

So what part of her news had set him off? The mention of Brenda's name? After three years, was the hurt still that fresh? Or was it that he still had feelings for her? They'd been a day away from the altar, after all.

The thoughts got shoved aside as she picked her way across a shallow spot in the Gooseberry, jabbing the end of her pole into the river-smoothed pebbles. Seth had switched to "The Happy Wanderer," and the rest of the group joined in. Yvonne's clear, sweet soprano carried the melody. April added her so-so voice to the mix—"Val-deri, Val-dera"—glad there was no one in front of her to offend. It kept her mind off Seth's strange behavior until the last line. "*Oh, may I always laugh and sing*". . . . Something about it hit her strangely. Maybe it was the word "always." Had she made it clear enough to Seth that she had no intention of letting this job interfere with their relationship, that her weekends would belong to him?

If it wouldn't cause a seven-hiker pileup, she'd stop right there in the middle of the trail and wrap her arms around him, whispering things for his ears only. *This won't change what's starting between us. If it's God's will, we'll make it work. We'll find time to be together. I promise I won't put my career ahead of you.*

She stumbled on a tree root, caught her balance again. Was that true? If he asked her not to take the job, to stay at KPOG forever just to be close to him, would she? Should she?

A rustling sound up ahead stopped her. She held her hand over her head and heard footsteps halt. Two whitetail deer stepped into the path, looked at her, then went back to the thick grass on the side of the trail. Stealthily, Seth's arms wrapped around her from behind. His warm breath tickled her ear.

"I'm sorry. I'm really happy for you." His lips grazed her cheek. "It'll all work out."

৵

Did he really believe any of what he'd just said? Seth's eyes tracked the doe and her yearling, but his mind was on the wisps of sun-kissed hair tickling his cheek. The paradox between the setting and his emotions spun his world off kilter. The rush of water over rocks in the distance, the dappled pattern created by sunlight filtering through the leaves, the smell of her hair, the camaraderie of a day with other believers. . .all clashed now with the havoc in his mind.

What was Brenda up to? He was so close to breaking all ties with her. Was this her parting shot? She wasn't happy, so she'd see to it that he wasn't either?

Behind him, Yvonne sneezed. The doe startled and skittered into the trees, her little one right behind her, taking with them his excuse for standing in the middle of the trail with his arms draped around the woman with golden hair. As they followed the trail east toward the lake, Seth went back to his brooding. Trying to make sense of Brenda Cadwell wasn't the best use of his brainpower, but he couldn't let it go. If he could figure out her motive, he'd know what to do. There was no way he was going to sit by idly and watch April get hurt.

He examined the possibilities as they came to him. Brenda had done some consulting work for television and radio stations over the years—"vision creating," as she called it. So maybe that's what this was. Maybe.

One thing he was certain of—she wasn't doing it altruistically to advance the career of the new love interest of the guy who dumped her at the altar. But she could be opening doors for April in hopes that other doors would slam in Seth's face.

It boiled down to two theories: She was either doing it to advance her own career. . .or to hurt him. And yet, it might still be the best thing for April. Until he knew more, he'd be the encourager she needed him to be.

❧

"I'm. . .happy for you."

April stared at Jill's pitiful attempt at a smile. Would everyone she told say those same words with equal fakeness? When she'd given her notice for the apartment, Sydney's enthusiasm had been just as artificial as Jill's. Yvonne, thankfully, hadn't even pretended to be happy for her. "Thank you."

"Your listeners will miss you. I'll miss you." Jill's usually perfect posture rounded to the curve of her chair. "You're building up quite a fan base in this little town, you know. People feel like you connect with them—and connect them to each other." Her red-nailed hand pressed against her black blouse. "You get to the heart, April."

Tears constricted April's throat. "Is this just you being weirdly emotional, or is this you doing your guilt-tripping manager job?"

"Both. I know I've always said I wanted to see you living up to your potential. Selfishly, I just hoped it would be right here. Have you prayed about this, long and hard?"

"Yes." The ghost of a doubt floated through her consciousness, but she shooed it away. She had spent much of the past week thanking God for opening this door and asking Him to help her put together a show that would honor Him and touch lives. She'd prayed her way through her tour of KOEK, through every word in the contract before she'd signed it. And yet, second thoughts had hovered for days. But that was normal. Anyone making changes this big would have a few doubts.

"Well then, I guess, like Scuffy the tugboat, you were meant for bigger things, and the rest of us will just have to live without you." Jill pulled a tissue from a carved black dispenser and blew her nose. "I'll get to work finding someone to fill your slot. I'm not going to say replacement, because I don't think we'll find anyone to do that."

❧

"Oh, baby, I'm so happy for you."

April pulled the phone away and stared at it before resting it back on her ear. Finally, a voice that actually matched the words. But from the strangest source. She closed her office door. "Thanks, Mom."

"It's what you've always wanted. My little girl, a TV talk show host! Wait till I tell my friends."

Friends? Was the woman whose words were bouncing off a satellite and into her office really her mother? "It's just a cable station. Not national syndication."

"But it's a start. And you'll have your weekends free so you can spend some time with me."

More guilt. April stared at the Itasca State Park wallpaper beneath the icons on her desktop. She didn't even remember telling her mother what her new hours would be. "Sure. . . some of the time. I'll be coming back here a lot."

Silence. A tight-sounding inhale. "It's a long drive from wher. . .ever you're going."

"I know." Only too well. Three hours hadn't seemed like much until she'd told Seth about the job offer. Six hours of driving every week. Would that get old? Would he get tired of only seeing her on weekends? Would she?

"Don't expect that man to wait around for you while you figure out your life." A tired sigh. "They never do."

sixteen

The new girl, the one Jill refused to call "April's replacement," was catching on faster than April would have thought. Chrissy Leibner was fresh out of school and as bouncy as Tigger. But her three-toned blond hair and fast, breathy words gave the wrong impression. After four days with her, April was astonished by her emotional and spiritual maturity. Jill had chosen well.

And it bugged April.

"Good job, Chrissy."

The Thursday afternoon spot, Chrissy's first solo on-air shift, had just finished. Her transitions had been smooth and witty.

"It's really an honor to work with you, April." Chrissy set her headphones on the desk." I looked up KPOG on the Internet. People love your show." Her pert little nose wrinkled. "That's not all they're talking about."

"I don't have time to read blogs. Do I want to know what people are saying?"

"They're talking about a guy who keeps calling your show and whether or not he's the Channel Five weatherman. Some people think there's a thing between you two. Is there?"

"Is that what they think?" April stood, hugging her laptop to her chest. "Let's call it a day."

❧

Brenda was eight minutes late.

April did a mini–drum solo on the tablecloth as she memorized the Sage Stoppe's menu. *Whole grilled lemon sole with lemongrass butter, roast cod with spring onion mash and soy butter sauce, rib eye steak with béarnaise sauce, and thin cut—*

"You must be April."

Dark eyes, olive skin, and thick, shampoo-commercial mahogany hair. The almost-wedding picture had not done Brenda Cadwell justice. April took the bangle-crowned hand and shook it, wondering as she did how the woman's fingers could be icy with the outside temperature nudging ninety.

"Thank you for taking the time, Brenda."

"My pleasure. It's so much easier to ask questions in person, isn't it?"

April nodded, suddenly wondering which one of them would be asking the questions. She'd been trying for a week to set up a meeting with Brenda and KOEK's station manager, who'd been out of town when she'd toured the station. When Brenda finally returned one of her many calls, she'd said it would work best for her to meet in Pine Bluff on Friday. She had some "business near there." The manager, apparently, was an extremely busy man.

April smiled, covering her irritation. "How was the drive?"

"Oh, you know how it is. Well, maybe you don't, living up here where there isn't any traffic."

"I went to school and worked in the Cities."

"You did, didn't you?" Brenda picked up the menu. "What's good here?"

"The fish chowder is to die for."

"Sounds heavy. I'll have a salad."

Their waitress, in a white apron and traditional Cornish bonnet, approached them and took Brenda's order first.

"I'll have the spinach salad with grilled chicken instead of the bacon. No croutons. Dressing on the side. And a glass of Perrier." She pushed her water goblet to the edge of the table.

"There will be an extra charge for the chicken."

Brenda's fingers fluttered. "Of course."

The young waitress nodded and smiled as she scribbled. "And how about you, Miss Douglas? Sorry we don't have chocolate fondue." She winked. "I heard you guys were getting serious," she whispered.

"My life is a fishbowl, Sherry." April winked back. "So the chowder would be fitting."

"Cup or bowl?"

"Make it a bowl. And can we have a bread basket with extra butter?"

Sherry headed for the kitchen, and April opened her notebook. Her lips parted, but Brenda spoke first.

"I bet you haven't been able to sleep a wink or talk about anything but your new show."

"I've got pages of ideas and questions. Some of them can probably only be answered by the people I'll be directly working with."

Brenda's thumbnail creased the crisply pressed fold of the cloth napkin next to her plate. "Mr. Palmer will be back next week. He took his daughter on a graduation trip to Italy."

"Seems strange that he'd hire somebody he hadn't met." There, she'd verbalized the loudest question in her head.

A corner of the cloth napkin bent under Brenda's finger. The long nail creased it, again and again. "He trusts me. So. . . is Seth excited about your new opportunity?"

I wouldn't exactly call it excitement. "Of course. He's even come up with some suggestions."

Brenda took a long draught of the lemon water she'd pushed aside earlier. "Knowing Seth, I imagine his vision is probably a little more 'out there' than what you'll be doing." She laughed and dabbed her lips with her napkin.

"What do you mean?" April rubbed her right thumb against her left.

"If Seth were to design a show for you, I don't think you'd have the kind of freedom you need, April."

"What do you think he'd do to squelch my 'freedom'?"

"He'd insist that your guests all be Christians whose stories have happy endings. As you and I know, that kind of format would turn away a lot of potential viewers."

April leaned forward on her elbows. "When we spoke on the phone. . .you. . ." She let the sentence trail off when she realized that Brenda's wide brown eyes were fixed on something other than her.

"Seth!" Though their tones were as different as night and day, both women spoke in tandem. "What are you doing here?"

❧

If protecting April meant making her mad, so be it. If protecting April meant making Brenda mad. . .he smiled extra-wide as he shook her cold fingers and pulled out the chair next to April. On the way to the restaurant, he'd thought back to the Sunday school lesson on the twelfth chapter of Romans he'd facilitated back in May—*Do not repay anyone evil for evil. Be careful to do what is right in the eyes of everybody.*

Lord, change my heart.

It was tempting to pretend he wasn't there for what both women knew he was. But that would have fallen short of doing what was right in the eyes of everybody. "I have a few questions about April's new job."

He'd known ahead of time that April's reaction could have gone either way, so he was disappointed, but not surprised, when her lips curved up but her eyes held no sparkle. He'd seen that look before. Brenda, wearing the smile he'd seen her practice in the vanity mirror in his car, turned to April. "Are you comfortable with him being here?"

"Of course."

She could have just said yes. She could have hesitated. "Of course" was a good sign. The waitress approached and asked in a giggly voice if he was ready to order. He asked for coffee and said he'd just order dessert when the women did, knowing full well that in Brenda's mind sugar was lumped in with the seven deadly sins.

April turned to him. "We haven't had a chance to get to my questions yet. Maybe yours will be answered at the same time mine are."

Was that a nice way of telling him to be quiet? Not a problem. He had no intention of monopolizing the conversation or making April feel inadequate in any way. He just wanted to be sure that Brenda didn't evade. Brenda was an expert evader. For the thousandth time, he wondered why he'd put up with that until it was almost too late. He smiled at April and then turned it on Brenda. "Great."

"What I want to talk about is format. Everything else was clearly outlined in the contract." April picked up her pen and pulled off the cap. "How involved are you in programming?" In a seemingly unconscious gesture, April shoved the cap back on her pen. "I called the station yesterday." She stared, letting her words sink in. "Until then, I was under the impression that you worked for KOEK."

A 100-watt smile beamed at April. "I do work *for* the station. I'm not employed on-site."

"So you're a consultant?"

Brenda took a sip—and then another—from her half-finished water glass. "Among other things, I'm a recruiter. When Seth told me about your idea for a show, I knew just where you were needed." The megasmile flipped from April to Seth and back again. "So let me hear your ideas, April. We need to start brainstorming about promotion."

Seth had had enough. His fingers closed around the handle of his butter knife, and he pointed it at Brenda. But just as his lips formed the first letter, April leaned forward. "I need some details. This is all way too vague for my comfort, Brenda. The pay is better than I'd expected, and the benefits are wonderful, but now that I know you're not employed at KOEK, I've got some huge concerns. I need to see in writing the things you promised—that I'll be in charge of picking my own guests, my own topics. And I need to know now."

Way to go, April. Seth high-fived her in his head. As soon as he had the chance, he'd apologize for barging in. Clearly, his presence wasn't needed at this meeting. This girl could hold her own.

Brenda nodded. "I'd have the same concerns if I were you." She bent down and pulled a tube of lipstick out of her purse, applying it without need of a mirror.

He'd forgotten how much that irritated him. "Brenda, just spell it out for her." April didn't need a knight on a white charger, but he couldn't help trying to play the role.

"I understand what—" Music blared from the floor near Brenda's feet. She closed the lipstick tube and picked up her purse, sliding her hand in and out. "Excuse me." She slid the cover up on her slim ruby red phone. "Hello. Oh no. Of course. No, not a problem. I'm on my way." Her lip did the fake pouty thing he'd once found so appealing. "I'm so, so sorry. I have to run." Her hand reached across the table to April. "I'll call you on Tuesday."

Her elegant hand reached out to him. "So good to see you, Seth. I'm so sorry I can't stay, but we'll talk soon." Her smile could melt lead. But it didn't touch him.

With her fingers in his grasp, he stared, letting her know he'd seen right through her. "Lots of big emergencies in the television business, aren't there?"

Her eyes glazed him before she pivoted on spiky heels and strode out.

The waitress appeared with their coffee and Brenda's bottled water. Seth stood up and moved to the vacated chair across from April and slid his coffee cup toward him as he asked the confused waitress what Brenda had ordered.

"Spinach salad, dressing on the side, no croutons, chicken breast instead of bacon." The girl in the apron and massive bonnet seemed to be struggling to rattle off the instructions in an even voice. Apparently, she'd sized up Brenda in short order.

"Heap on some bacon and pour the dressing on top, and I'll eat it." He turned his attention on April. "Mind if I join you for lunch?"

April looked as though she'd just stepped off the Tilt-A-Whirl at the county fair. "I. . .guess." Parallel lines formed above her nose. "That remark about emergencies was rude."

"Yes, it was. I had every intention of being polite, but. . . ." He lifted his coffee cup. "If I were a betting man, I'd bet there was nobody on the other end when her phone rang."

"Seth!"

It was the second time she'd used his name in half an hour. Was he ever going to hear her say it again without the exclamation point? "Brenda downloaded a program that rings your phone to get you out of sticky situations. She hit the 'hot key' when she reached for her lipstick."

"You don't know that for sure."

Oh yes, I do. "Did anything get settled in your mind in that. . . brief encounter?"

"No."

He didn't like seeing her embarrassed. He put both hands around his cup to keep from touching her hand in a gesture she might perceive as patronizing. "So what's next on the dream list?"

"Thank you." A genuine smile lit her eyes. So he'd been right to change the subject. "I have to put off anything that costs money since it's going to cost me something to move. . . ."

"Can we leave that little fact out of our conversation? I'm being an ostrich on that subject."

The waitress appeared with a bowl of soup, a bread basket, and Seth's salad. When she left, April reached across the table and held her hands out for his. "I'll pray."

Her warm hands hugged his. "Lord God, thank You for

this food and this time. Thank You for the way You meet all our needs. You are in the details, Lord, and we trust You."

She opened her eyes and the deepness of the blue was once again too deep, but he couldn't have let go of her hands if his life depended on it—nor could he remember what they'd been talking about before she'd reached for his hands. He fumbled for a coherent sentence. "Will you make it home in time to watch the weather tonight?"

Her thumbs swept across his knuckles. "I always make it home in time for you."

seventeen

April's head felt like it was banded with steel straps. She kicked off her shoes and dropped her purse next to Snow Bear. With little to do other than supervise Chrissy, the afternoon had dragged. Her headache, which had started the moment Brenda walked out of the Sage Stoppe without answering a single question, had gotten worse with each jerk of the second hand on her office clock. And just to add to the stress, she'd promised to spend Saturday with her mother.

She turned on the window air conditioner in the bedroom and positioned a fan so that it would draw the cool air into the living room. Even Willy and Splash looked wilted. "Hard to fight in this heat, isn't it?" Neither of them looked especially anxious to grab the flakes she sprinkled over them. "I know just how you feel."

After changing into shorts, she rummaged through the refrigerator for something that wouldn't require heat or effort. Thanks to the generosity of a listener who worked for Bridgeman's, two pints of Wolf Tracks ice cream called her name through the freezer door, but she settled on a cold chicken leg and some cottage cheese.

Paper plate and iced tea in hand, she flopped onto the couch and turned on the news. Five minutes to Seth. The thought revived a little voice she'd been trying to silence all afternoon. Why hadn't he asked her to do something tonight? Not that she wanted to be locked into a Friday night date routine, but he hadn't mentioned any plans. She sank back on Snow Bear as she took a halfhearted bite of chicken. The bear's head turned when she squished him. He seemed to be staring at her.

"Tell me he's not with Brenda." Was Seth the "business" Brenda had in Pine Bluff?

A tap on the door kept her from waiting for an answer from a stuffed bear. "Come on in."

Yvonne's shift at the nursing home had ended more than two hours earlier, but she was still in uniform.

"What have you been up to?" When she didn't get an answer, April looked closer. Yvonne's eyes were red and puffy. "What's wrong?"

"We lost a resident a little while ago. A sweet little old lady." Yvonne dropped her purse on the floor and closed the door behind her. "And then on the way home, Michael W. Smith was singing 'Friends,' and I just started thinking about how nothing's for sure, you know, and nothing's going to be the same after you move. I know you'll come back here on weekends, but you'll want to be with Seth, and I'll be married in two months and—" A sob shook her shoulders.

April jumped up and wrapped her arms around Yvonne, triggering her own flood of tears. When she pulled away, Yvonne laughed. "Do I look as bad as you do?"

Staring at the streaks of black that ran from Yvonne's eyes to her chin, April shook her head. "You could never look as bad as me. Do you have plans tonight?"

"Not until eight. Kirk's having dinner with some guys from work."

"Have a seat. I know just what we need."

Seth was pointing at a radar map when April sat down beside Yvonne with two spoons and two pints of Wolf Tracks. Listening to Seth's smooth voice, April shut out the uncertainty of the day. "This is kind of the best of everything, you know? My headache's going away already."

"Just what the doctor ordered." Yvonne's raccoon eyes squinted when she smiled. "The guy's not hard to look at."

Seth's brown sports jacket matched his eyes. April tuned in

and out of the weather report.

". . .line of storms headed our way that'll give us a break from the heat for the Fourth of July weekend, but we'll have to be on the lookout for possible severe weather. This is the kind of front that could develop. . . ."

"He's so sweet." April licked her spoon like a Popsicle.

"Told you so."

"Yes, you did." She pulled her attention off Seth's eyes and onto his words.

". . .All in all, it's a good night to do something in air-conditioned comfort. Something like the climbing wall at the YMCA in Coon Rapids, maybe." His dimple deepened. "This is Seth Bachelor for KXPB Weather. Have a blessed night." His index finger pointed at the camera. "I'll be over to pick you up at seven."

Yvonne gave a long, low whistle. "I told you so."

❧

The gym smelled of stale sweat and dirty socks. Oldies music and the triumphant yells of three teens who'd made it to the top rebounded off the cement-block walls. April stood at the bottom of the climbing wall in full harness, telling herself the dampness on her palms was irrational. One of the spotters had told her the wall was twenty-eight feet tall, only a fraction of the height of the water tower. But the water tower had ladder rungs, and it didn't have a four-foot overhang at the top,

"This'll be a piece of cake for you." Seth double-checked her harness.

"It's not only fear of heights I'm battling; it's fear of no biceps."

Seth pinched her upper arm between his thumb and fingers. "Hm. You may be right."

"Thanks for the confidence."

He tousled her hair the way he'd done with Wesley. "One step at a time."

"One step at a time. One step at a time." She whispered the words as her fingertips found a hold above her head and her foot left the floor.

Rock by rock, with Seth only two feet away, offering a constant flow of encouragement, she made it to the overhang. "I think this is far enough for the first time."

"You have to at least try it. Even if you do slip, you won't hit the ground."

"But I'll dangle like a spastic spider."

His laugh bounced off the rock face. "I think I have just the thing to get you over the top. Stay right there."

His left hand stretched toward a rock that jutted out just above her head. He found a foothold and shifted to his left until his arm touched hers. "I've been trying to figure out the best time to break this to you."

If he thought he was calming her jitters, he was way off base. "Break what to me?"

"Well, you see"—his lips grazed her knuckles—"it appears I'm in love with you."

❧

"Take your shoes off." April padded up the weather-beaten outside stairs leading to her mother's apartment. Her stomach felt jittery. Maybe having Seth bring her to her mother's wasn't such a great idea after all. She wouldn't have a getaway car if things got tense, and she'd have to worry about Seth staying awake on the hour drive back to Pine Bluff.

Shoes in hand, Seth followed. "Are we gonna get in trouble for breaking curfew?"

"Shh! Want me to get grounded?"

"I thought you said your feet wouldn't touch the ground for days." He nuzzled her cheek with his nose as she fit the key in the lock and opened the door to the galley kitchen.

Seth set her gym bag on the floor. April looked up at him. Slits of light from a streetlamp sneaked through the venetian blinds and lined his face. She slid easily into his arms, feeling like she belonged there. "Thank you," she whispered against his shirt.

"What did I do now?"

"I was feeling so sorry for myself, sitting home alone on a Friday night after a lousy day, and here you had the whole night planned. The climb, dinner, the walk, the words. . ."

"Which words?" His chest vibrated as his words baited her.

"I love you."

"You do?"

"I do."

He pulled back several inches, one arm still around her waist. The fingers of his right hand glided into her hair. "Even if it means a three-hour drive, I'm going to keep filling up your Friday nights. If that's okay with you, of course."

"That's o—" The overhead light flashed on.

"April!" Her mother stood in the doorway in a faded pink robe, gray roots showing in her tangled hair, clutching a vacuum cleaner wand like a billy club. "What is *he* doing here?"

Pulling slightly away from Seth, April kept her hand on his back. "Mom, I'd like you to meet Seth. Seth, this is my mother, Lois Douglas."

Seth extended his hand and then dropped it to his side when the gesture wasn't reciprocated. "Nice to meet you, Mrs. Douglas."

"It's two in the morning."

April commanded her eyes not to roll. "I told you I'd be here late."

"You told me *you'd* be here late."

"We were at the Y, and then we had dinner at Solera." Why did she feel like a high school kid caught sneaking home after midnight?

"The couch is made up." Her mother turned and stepped into the dining room. "I doubt I'll be able to go back to sleep now."

Was that remark made to incite guilt or to say she'd be watching to make sure Seth wasn't staying?

Seth's hand slipped from her back. "Mrs. Douglas? Could I talk to you for a moment?"

April's mother stopped as if his words were a brick wall. "Nothing you can say will change a thing, Mr. Bachelor."

"I know that. I'm so sorry about the loss of your daughter. We never would have taken her if we'd known she was so sick. She turned in the permission slip, so—"

Lois Douglas's hands rose to her face. "I don't remember signing it. If I'd known she'd be outside, that she'd get wet and cold. . ." Her face distorted, and she turned away.

April covered the space in three strides and put her arms around her mother. She looked up into Seth's helpless face, and they stood like that, eyes locked, until her mother's sobs quieted. April guided her to a straight-backed chair and left the room to find a box of tissues.

When she returned, Seth was on his knees in front of her mother.

". . .anyone's fault, Mrs. Douglas. From what April has told me, Caitlyn was a pretty headstrong girl."

Seth's words were soft. Unbelievably, her mother responded with a smile. "She was that."

"Can I tell you about that day?"

Her mother took a Kleenex, wiped her face, and nodded.

April watched in awe as Seth, still on his knees, described driving toward the bank of dark clouds with three teens in the back of Darren's van singing Sesame Street songs.

"Your daughter was wearing this crazy elephant stocking cap."

Her mother nodded. "April bought it for her."

Tears stung April's eyes. Shortly before Caitlyn's diagnosis, they'd gone to see *Horton Hears a Who*. She could picture the floppy elephant ears so clearly. And Caitlyn's comical grin.

"When it started to rain, we pulled under an overpass and

dug out the rain gauges so the kids could set them out. Caitlyn took one of the gauges and ran out into a field." He paused and looked up at April.

April hadn't heard this part, but she nodded encouragement.

"She was laughing and leaping over the rows of cut corn with the other kids following her. My buddy made a comment that they were acting as goofy as his four-year-old with his little friends. All of a sudden, Caitlyn stopped." Again, he glanced up at April. "She raised her hands in the air like she was worshipping. Even from the road, I could see her smile. And then. . .she took off her cap. . .and threw it into the wind."

A gasp slipped from April's throat.

"It was. . .beautiful. And until that moment, we had no idea she was sick."

eighteen

He'd given Brenda long enough. Not one of his e-mails, text messages, or phone calls had been answered. Seth had no doubt where he'd find her at six o'clock on Thursday morning. She'd be working off the guilt from eating pizza at her Wednesday night book club.

He rubbed his hand over his face as he turned onto Spring Street. He was a morning person, but setting the alarm for four o'clock wasn't his idea of fun. He scanned the Anytime Fitness parking lot. Three spaces from the front door, he spotted the silver Audi. But instead of opening the car door, he closed his eyes.

Lord, let my words be pleasing to You. You know my heart is not filled with grace at this moment, but let me listen to You before I speak.

Two minutes later, he stood face-to-face with a sweaty, disheveled, and extremely self-conscious Brenda.

As the blush covered her cheeks and neck, she greeted him with a smile and a hug that he didn't return. "What a surprise! What are you doing here?"

"I just have a few questions." He lifted the two envelopes in his hand as a shield. "Does this job you've offered April really exist?"

"Of course! What do you take me for?"

Lord, help. . . . His teeth clamped down on his tongue until he could trust himself with words.

"Is there any part of this offer that isn't exactly the way you described it to her?"

"She'll be on the air with her own show in six weeks,

I promise." A manicured hand ran from his shoulder to his elbow. "You must be sooo proud of her."

Pins and needles prickled along his spine. "If you're lying about any of this, I'll be back." He hadn't intended to sound like the Terminator. Then again, he liked the sound of that title. That was, in fact, what he'd come to do.

"You'll always be back, Seth." Pink nails retraced the line from his elbow to shoulder.

Seth drew back. The muscles in his neck tightened like a vise. The envelopes in his hand felt suddenly heavy. He shoved the smaller one, the one addressed to her father, in front of her face. "This is the last payment. I need your signature on the deed, and this will all be behind us."

The color left her face. She blinked. And then her lips pulled tight across her teeth and her shoulders straightened. "There's no proof that you've given me a single penny for my half."

❧

The promised call from Brenda hadn't come. April had left messages five days in a row. She tossed her cell phone on her desk and her pencil holder in the cardboard box on the floor. She could recite the voice mail message by heart, flawlessly imitating the chirpy tone.

Plunking down on her desk chair, she stared at the KOEK home page, trying to picture her face on it. Picking up her phone, she did the thing Brenda had, with no explanation, told her not to do. She dialed the station and asked for the manager.

"Bud Palmer here."

"Mr. Palmer, this is April Douglas."

"Yes. I've been waiting for Brenda to set up a meeting with you."

April's shoulders lowered from their permanent place near her ears. He knew who she was. That eliminated her biggest fear, anyway. "Mr. Palmer, I've got tons of questions, and I imagine you have some for me. If you're busy right now, I'll call back when it's convenient."

"I'll make time right now. I'm excited about you coming. We put a half page ad in the *Winona Daily News* announcing the upcoming *On the Spot*."

"What's that?"

"Your. . .show." He sounded confused. "Brenda came up with the idea. Hasn't she told you anything? Yeah, *On the Spot*. Our tagline is 'Real People. Real Shockers.'"

April's throat constricted. "Wh. . .what is the format?"

"Just like it sounds. One guest per show. They sit there having coffee with you just like you're old buddies, and then *zam!* they let go a zinger, some buried secret or juicy bit of gossip about a friend, old boss, or ex—somebody they want to get even with." His laugh belonged in a circus sideshow. "And then you call that person on the phone and repeat what you just heard. The rest, as they say, is history."

Black splashes spattered across her field of vision. Her breath came in short, squeezed spurts. April lowered her head to her knees.

"April? Did I lose you? Hello?"

"Mr. Palmer. . ." Her fingers spasmed around the phone. "That's not. . .the job. . .I was offered."

⋟

There was a note on her door when she got home. *April—I found someone to rent the apartment on the 15th. Stop in to say good-bye and give me your address before you move. Sydney.*

She was jobless. In six days, she'd be homeless. She hadn't even found an apartment in Winona yet—not that she would have gone there now. April ripped down the note and kicked open the door. Bud Palmer's cackle echoed in her ears. *"Christian? You thought this was a Christian show? Where in the world did you get that idea?"*

Closing the door, she leaned against it. *Lord Jesus. . . .* It was the beginning and ending of her prayer, the same one she'd repeated over and over since breaking the phone connection with Bud Palmer. From the dim recesses of her memory, a verse whispered. . . . *"The Spirit helps us in our weakness. We do not know what we ought to pray for, but the Spirit himself intercedes for us with groans that words cannot express."*

Her purse dropped, her arms crossed over her waist. She hadn't yet shed a tear. Walking, driving, breathing sucked all her energy, not leaving enough to manufacture tears. She couldn't afford the luxury of giving in to self-pity yet. She should be doing something—making lists, searching the Internet, thinking. But thoughts wouldn't stick together in her mind.

Slowly, she opened her eyes and stared at the hodgepodge of boxes, bags, and baskets that cluttered her living room. Splash and Willy treaded water between two DVD skyscrapers. Snow Bear slept on a pile of folded blankets on the floor. . . like the street bear he was soon to be. Thin, late-afternoon sunlight hit the picture leaning against a box on the couch. Itasca. In the photograph, misty morning light filtering through the trees, reflecting in the water. The headwaters of the mighty Mississippi. . .quiet, serene. . .everything her life wasn't at the moment. A place of beginnings, a place to think, to sort through the remnants of what used to be her life. . .

She could pack tonight and be there by noon tomorrow. She'd miss her last day of work and the surprise going away party everyone had been whispering about. But maybe they'd be willing to postpone it until Monday. It wasn't like she was leaving town.

Like a shot of caffeine, the plan jolted her into action. Mental lists made lines and columns out of the mess that had filled her head just moments before. *Call Jill, cancel Winona hotel reservation, call Itasca, tell Yvonne, Mom, Seth. . . .*

Seth. Earlier, with Bud Palmer's laugh still ringing in her

ear, she'd picked up the phone to call him. And then it hit her. He'd feel responsible. He'd shared April's dream with Brenda, like handing her live ammunition. She had to tell him in person that she wasn't angry. He needed to see that she was doing okay.

Right.

As she bent to pick up her purse, a buzz sounded in the outside pocket. She pulled out her phone and stared at the caller ID. "Hi, Mom." She didn't have the energy to mask her mood.

"April?" Her voice sounded tight, strained. "I. . .heard you turned down the job in Winona."

Alarm bells went off in April's head. "Where did you hear that, and how did you know—"

"Did you get another job offer, honey?" Her voice bordered on shrill.

"No." Muffled sobs met her ear. *Not again, not now.* "What's going on, Mom? How did you—"

"It's all my fault!" A louder sob. "I thought it was the best thing. I thought it would be good for you to get away from. . . there."

Every cell in April's brain stood at attention. "What are you talking about?"

"I thought you'd love the new job. Brenda made it sound like it was perfect for you."

"*Brenda?*" April was yelling, but she didn't care. "You talked to Brenda?"

"It was weeks ago, before I met Seth. I was so worried about you. I wanted to know the truth about him, so I looked her up, and she said she had the perfect solution. . . ."

April's phone snapped shut.

❧

The last time she'd entered the doors of KXPB-TV, she'd been young and idealistic, with a head full of dreams. Before

Caitlyn died, before she got a great job and then threw it away like a dog with a bone in his mouth looking at his own reflection.

She stepped into the dimly lit empty reception area. No one sat at the two desks behind the counter. The screen saver on a monitor rolled and transposed the call letters. *KXPB. . . X-ceeding X-pectations.*

From somewhere in the back of the long, narrow building came the sound of the current broadcast. The news was over, and the seven-to-eight slot was filled with spotlights on local organizations and school functions. *Prime-Time Pine Bluff.*

If she hadn't seen Seth's Camry in the parking lot, she would have left. The quiet was eerie, and she had no idea where to find him. A blade of light from a doorway sliced across the darkened hallway in front of her. She walked toward it, stopping when she reached the door. MERVIN FULLER, STATION MANAGER, the nameplate read. She tapped on the door.

"Come on in."

The voice startled her. She pushed the door open. With his phone in one hand, pencil in the other, and feet crossed on top of the desk, Seth looked as surprised to see her as she was to see him.

"April!" His feet arced over the corner of the desk and hit the floor at the same time his phone landed in its cradle. "Hi!" He stood and walked toward her, hands reaching out before she reached him.

She thought she was smiling. But the look on Seth's face told her otherwise. His hands clamped on her arms. "Sit down." He guided her to a chair and took the one beside her. "What's wrong?"

The sobs gave no warning. Racking, jarring, they emanated from some buried storehouse of hurt and fear and longing.

Like a fortress, his arms surrounded her. Her face pressed

against his chest. He didn't talk, just held her tighter, stroked her hair. Never in her life had she been held like this. How many times as a little girl had she imagined a rescuer, someone who would step in and make things right, who would defend and protect her? God had been her strength, but still she'd craved the feel of strong arms around her. Over the thud of Seth's heart, she heard him whisper.

"Lord, comfort her, protect her, and fill her with Your love and the knowledge of Your presence." His fingers stroked her cheek. "Whatever it is, April, I'm here for you. We'll get through it. We'll work it out."

His words brought fresh tears. Finally, when his shirt was damp and her eyes sore, but there were no more tears, she told him.

&.

Seth eased off the accelerator when his headlights lit the sign for the 107A exit. He'd only been driving for about fifty minutes, but the muscles in his forearms ached from gripping the wheel. A sense of déjà vu washed over him. This was his second trip to St. Paul in fourteen hours.

But this time, he was hoping to *not* find Brenda.

As he turned onto the exit, his shirt pulled away from his chest then touched his skin again, cold and damp with April's tears. Saying good-bye had been so hard tonight. But the only way he could offer her any hope was to bring an end to his three years of bondage to the Miss-St.-Cloud-wannabe.

He took a right on 70th Street. Minutes later, he pulled into the circle driveway on Lone Oak Road and parked in front of two tall white columns. It was the first time he'd ever used the front door.

Chimes echoed behind double mahogany doors at the press of his finger against a lit button. The door swung open, and the woman who had almost become his mother-in-law stood before him. Openmouthed shock smoothed her face in a way

Botox never had. "Seth!"

"Margaret."

Perfectly tipped nails ran through short-cropped, eternally blond hair. "Are you. . .looking for Brenda?" A spark of hope lit her gray eyes.

"No." *Absolutely no.* "Is Gil home?"

Margaret tugged at the bottom of her fitted blouse. "He's in his office." She opened the door wider and stepped aside for him to pass. "I have raspberry lemonade."

He stopped. The sadness in her voice turned him around. "That would be good." He gave her a quick hug. Though she probably deserved most of the blame for the way her daughter had turned out, he doubted that she had any clue.

She led the way across marble floors and handwoven wool rugs to the study, stopping on the way to fill a chilled glass with lemonade.

Gil Cadwell stood in front of an arched window with his back to the door. In his midfifties, he was still a striking man. Disdain for golf carts kept him in shape.

"Hello, Gil."

The man whirled. "Seth!" A grin lit his face. He covered the space between them in four long strides and engulfed Seth in a bear hug. "It's been too long. Sit down." He pulled away and gestured to two overstuffed leather chairs. As they sat down, he said, "Got your check this afternoon. By courier—you must have been anxious to make that last payment. I imagine that feels mighty good. You're a prince of a guy, Mr. Bachelor. More of a man than I would have been at your age."

"Thank you. But. . .there's a little problem." Just imagining the look that would soon harden Gil's features started his stomach churning. If he'd known any other way to put this to rest, he wouldn't have involved the man who had been more of a father to him than his own father. "Brenda is refusing to sign over her half of the business."

"What?" Gil's eyes glinted like steel.

"I have nothing on paper to show that I paid her off."

Gil rose to his feet. His hands coiled in tight fists at his sides. "I'll take care of it, Seth. Enough is enough. She'll sign. You've done more than anyone would have expected." His shoulders suddenly lowered. Shame and frustration wove through a heavy sigh. "I'm so sorry, Seth."

Standing and closing the gap between them, Seth put his hand on the older man's shoulder. They'd had too many conversations about Gil Cadwell's oldest daughter. "It's not your fault." He pulled his hand away. "I just don't know what game she's playing this time. She doesn't want the station, does she?"

"No. She doesn't." A sad smile lifted one corner of Gil's mouth. "She wants you."

nineteen

As she turned north onto Main Street, sunlight shot between two buildings, through the passenger window, around Yvonne, and behind the frames of April's sunglasses. Her eyes and head still hurt from crying, and she had no more answers than she'd had the day before. And yet, a vague sense of hope had begun to infiltrate her dark mood. All because of a man who knew how to listen. . .and hug.

And a best friend. She squinted at Yvonne. "This may be the most sacrificial thing anyone's ever done for me."

"That's pitiful." An undecipherable smile twisted Yvonne's lips to the side. "I take a personal day from work to walk in the woods with you, and you call it sacrificing? You ain't seen nuttin' yet." She pointed ahead to the right. "Pull up in front of Perk Place. I want to stock up."

April parked the car in the shadow of the coffee shop awning and opened her purse. "Get me a Polar Cap."

"Come in with me." In answer to the question on April's face, Yvonne added, "I've only got two hands."

Closing her purse, April got out and followed, muttering the whole way. "We're stopping for brunch in Brainerd, you know. You've got three bags of chips and half a dozen water bottles in the backseat. How much stuff do you need for a four-hour trip?"

Yvonne walked ahead of her to the counter, ignoring every question April aimed at her back. A boy with three earrings in one ear asked for her order.

"I'll have a large Polar Cap, a medium White Chocolate Mocha with a squirt of raspberry, a large Dolce Latte sprinkled with cinnamon, and a large Hazelnut decaf, cream on the side."

April folded her arms across her chest. "How many rest areas do you think there are between here and Itasca?" She turned away, staring at booth after booth of tourists with cameras, hats, and rambunctious children. Yvonne grabbed her elbow.

"Do you want a muffin or a scone?" Yvonne's finger jabbed the air in the direction of a glass-front case. "Pick one, my treat."

"I'll have a chocolate chip muffin."

"Make that four."

"Yvonne! You'll be a whopping size 2 by Sunday if you don't watch it."

Yvonne handed money to the earringed boy and took a white bag from him. Motioning for April to wait at the pickup window, she waved. "I'll be in the car."

Rude. Something was eating at Yvonne. Probably some misunderstanding with Kirk. Before they got to Milaca, she'd wrangle the truth out of her. April took the cardboard holder with the four drinks and walked toward the door. With one foot on the sidewalk, she nearly dropped the cups.

Yvonne leaned against the side of April's car, holding the bag of muffins and smiling like a Cheshire cat. To her right was Kirk.

To her left stood a man with deep brown eyes. . .holding out a jar of jam and a package of Twinkies.

"Breakfast?"

੨ঽ

Towering red pines, ramrod straight, stood like sentinels on either side of the needle-covered path. They walked past a cabin built by the Civilian Conservation Corps in the 1930s. Huge brown-painted logs stood on a stone foundation. A stone chimney rose from the roof. Cozy, romantic. . . A warm flush started at April's ears and spread toward her toes.

Pulling her sweatshirt off, she tied it around her waist, relishing the sun on her bare arms, the slight breeze drying her damp T-shirt. She slipped her hand back into Seth's. "Have I said 'Thank you' lately?"

"Not in the last three minutes. So we're forgiven for wrecking your girl time?" He pointed toward Kirk and Yvonne, walking hand in hand far ahead of them.

Why was it, again, that two days at Itasca with Yvonne had sounded so wonderful? *You can wreck my girl time any day.* "You're forgiven. I just feel bad about the dumpy motel you guys are stuck with while we're in the lodge."

"We guys is tough." He gave a manly grunt. "It's only one night. And we'll get our share of time in front of the fireplace at the lodge when that front comes in this afternoon. We're in for quite a storm." His thumb caressed the back of her hand. "How are you doing, for real? Or would you rather not talk about it?"

"I'm still a little numb. God's got this all figured out. I know that. I'm trying to look at this as an adventure into the unknown."

"That's my girl!"

She liked the sound of those words.

Inches off the path, a patch of sunlight illuminated a lady's slipper. Delicate white petals hung suspended over a pink-tinged pouch. A low hum drew her gaze to a circle of ferns. Low above the deep green fronds, a dragonfly hovered, its blue body held aloft by clear, black-veined wings that beat the air. All reminders to savor the moment.

Seth let go of her hand. His arm slid across her shoulders, unspoken encouragement for her to open up.

"I've had plenty of panic moments in the past twenty-four hours, but I don't think the full truth has sunk in yet. I don't have a job. I don't have a place to live. I'm going to end up sleeping on my mother's couch and busing tables at a greasy spoon, all because, once again, I checked my reporter instincts at the door."

"Please tell me you're not blaming yourself for this."

"I'm too trusting."

Pine needles absorbed the sound of Seth's laugh. "That's not a fault, April. You're not a cynic, and that's commendable. You were up against a master of deception. Believe me, I know."

They stopped at the sign for the headwaters. Kirk and Yvonne were already balancing on the rocks that crossed the shallow water. Acutely aware that Seth seemed to be gathering his thoughts, April read the sign half-consciously: HERE 1475 FT ABOVE THE OCEAN THE MIGHTY MISSISSIPPI BEGINS TO FLOW ON ITS WINDING WAY 2552 MILES TO THE GULF OF MEXICO.

"If I hadn't told Brenda about your dream, this never would have happened."

April pulled back and stared into his eyes. "Please tell me you're not blaming yourself for this."

A wink accompanied his smile. His hands rose to her face. "I helped get you into this mess. If you'll let me, I'd like to be part of the solution."

&

"Maybe we shouldn't go all the way to the top." Gripping the railings on either side of her, April yelled above the wind.

"Go on down if you want." Seth's voice came from behind her.

And give in to fear. She shook her head and nailed her gaze to the backs of Yvonne's knees. *I can do this.* She didn't dare look up but figured there couldn't be more than three more zigzag flights of stairs to the top of the eighty-foot Aiton Heights fire tower. The view at the top would be worth it. It would.

The wind seemed to pick up with each step. The tower swayed, slightly but unnervingly. Finally, she planted her feet in the green-painted, seven-foot-square roofed cab at the top.

She walked across the platform and stood beside Yvonne. "Wow." Thousands of acres of trees spread in every direction. A blue lake rested like a sapphire amid the green. To their right, the sky was deep blue and cloudless, but black clouds rolled toward them from the southwest.

Seth came up behind her and wrapped his arms around her. "You stared down another fear. This could get to be a habit, you know."

The temperature was dropping, and his warmth was welcome. She nestled against his chest. "Next week, bungee jumping."

She felt, rather than heard, the rumble of his laugh. "I'll be the one on the ground taking pictures."

April pointed toward the mountain of steel gray clouds roiling and tumbling, growing taller and wider before their eyes. "It's moving fast."

"We'd better get back down." Seth's arms dropped. "Hold on. I've got a call."

April turned, watching the expression on his face as he answered the call. His eyes glowed. "Uh-huh. You're sure? Okay, I'll ask her."

His eyes fixed on hers as he closed the phone. A ripple of fear swept over April, though she had no idea why.

"That was Darren." Seth's hand grasped her arm, as if to steady her. "About that fear-conquering habit. . ."

&

The minute the van door closed behind her, she knew she'd made a huge mistake. By the time she found the words to explain her change of mind, Darren was peeling out of the gas station parking lot. April pressed her hand against the window, in final farewell to Kirk and Yvonne. She stared at her car, with Kirk sliding in behind the wheel, until Darren turned a corner on what felt like two wheels. She was trapped.

Next to her in the center of the middle seat, oblivious to her terror, Seth dug around in a camera bag, familiarizing himself with different lenses. Darren, his eyes more on the conglomeration of equipment in the passenger seat than on the road, jabbered with Seth in a language April didn't understand. Terms like "supercell," "radial velocity," "A-bomb," "agitated region," "wedge," "altocumulus," "knuckles," and "anvil" ricocheted off the van's interior.

April's fingers melded into her shoulder harness. They were heading west, barreling toward an enormous wall of gray. The sky took on a bile green hue. Wind rocked the van. Veins stood out on Darren's hands as he fought with the steering wheel.

Seth unfastened his seat belt and reached between the front seats. Swiveling Darren's laptop so that April could see the screen, he pointed to an angry blob of red and orange on the radar. "There's hail in there. Figuring in that updraft, I'm guessing it's big. Golf ball–size at least." The zeal in his voice made him sound more like a sportscaster than a meteorologist. He sat on the edge of the seat, hands folded, eyes darting between the radar and the windshield. "Yeah, baby. This is gonna be good."

Good? What planet were these guys from? Maybe the account in Genesis had been mistranslated. The thing God took out of man to form into woman wasn't a rib; it was common sense!

But that didn't explain Caitlyn. Though she'd been a basketball whiz, April's sister had also been as girlie girl as they come. And yet, the only thing she'd underlined twice on her dream list had been "See a tornado." So what would Caitlyn be doing if she were here. . .sitting next to tall, dark, and handsome, speeding toward a whirling bank of violent clouds? The answer startled her. Caitlyn would be laughing.

So maybe April couldn't laugh, but she could make an effort to relax and to try to understand the man beside her. "What did Mark Twain say again?"

His lips parted in a look that she could only label "delight." "'Courage is not the absence of fear but resistance to the mastery of fear.'"

"What's the rest of it?"

"'Except a creature be part coward, it is not a compliment to say it is brave.'" He laughed, wrapped both arms around her, and planted a noisy kiss on her cheek. "You're amazing."

Her eyes opened wide. "Amazingly scared."

"Amazing *because* you're scared. And you're here."

&

"Listen to the roar!" Seth lowered his window.

Pressure pounded against April's eardrums. The noise was like nothing she'd ever experienced. Like standing directly beneath Niagara Falls.

On top of the roar, the heavens opened fire on them, on the acres of ripening corn on either side of the highway. Hail, bouncing like ping-pong balls, bombarded the van with a thundering volume that drowned out the voice of the radio announcer.

The barrage lasted only moments. The deafening noise stopped as abruptly as it started, leaving a silence equally disturbing. Darren turned north onto Highway 169. The greenish sky gave way to murky black. Beside her, Seth ducked even lower for a better view through the windshield.

April crouched beside him, waiting, her heart pounding with something that wasn't fear alone. Excited anticipation had somehow sneaked in. The realization stunned her.

"There!" She followed Seth's outstretched hand to a V-shaped cloud descending from a swirling, pewter gray mass. Suddenly, a white tube dropped like a massive Slinky.

"What a hose!"

"That's a monster!"

"Look at the motion at the base. Huge debris cloud!"

Seth's and Darren's words overlapped. From the van radio,

stern warnings added to the chaos: ". . . long line of storms moving northeast at about thirty miles per hour. We do not want you to be out looking at this potentially hazardous storm. There are spotters on the ground, emergency management directors and trained spotters. Stay indoors. Seek shelter. If you're out in this, do not stay in your car. Do not park under an overpass. Find a low-lying ditch and lie flat until the storm passes. The storm center is heading toward Hill City and. . . ."

Shingles, branches, fence posts, and corn stalks spun out from the dust-choked vortex that ripped across the open fields. Narrowing in the middle, the tornado was shaped more like a bud vase than a funnel. April watched in stunned silence, a sense of awe momentarily obliterating her fear. She glanced at the speedometer. The needle edged toward eighty. Darren made a wide turn onto a gravel road, barreling toward the next intersection where he again headed north.

"Incredible! Turn off the wipers for a minute." Seth aimed the video camera at the white shaft that seemed to hover on the road about two miles ahead of them, churning a brown cloud of debris, spitting out trees like toothpicks. "Great shot. Great. . ." He lowered the camera, leaned forward. "Darren. . ." His voice was thick with warning.

"I see it." Darren slammed on the brakes.

"Back up! Get out of here! It's headed straight for us!"

April's hands clamped onto Seth's arm as the van sped backwards.

"We're okay. We're safe." Seth repeated the words, but his face told the truth.

A piece of PVC pipe smashed against the windshield. Seconds later, the brown cloud engulfed the van. Darren slowed. Something heavy crashed against the roof. Seth grabbed a jacket from the backseat and threw it over her. April knew instinctively why. To shield her from breaking glass. She squeezed her eyes shut and buried her face in his shoulder.

Just when April was sure she would scream, silence slammed down on them.

Dust settled. The twister had disappeared. A whoop from Darren shattered the stillness. Seth echoed the sound and then broke into laughter. As relief flooded her body, April pried her fingers from Seth's arm.

Darren did a U-turn and then came to a stop. Sunlight knifed through steel gray clouds. A swath of color arced from the split in the clouds to a field of gently fluttering corn.

Seth's lips brushed her ear. "I'm in love with one mighty brave lady."

twenty

Seth stood at a distance, watching as April got down on her knees beside a little girl with windswept blond ringlets and spoke into the KXPB microphone.

"While her mom fills out Red Cross vouchers for food and new clothes, I'm visiting with three-year-old Zoe Lewis. Zoe and her mom and little sister moved into a mobile home park just outside of Hinckley only two months ago." April looked from the camera to the little girl and back. "In the wake of a series of tornadoes that touched down in Minnesota a week ago, Zoe's family is homeless, and Zoe's holding the only possession the Lewis family now owns." She jiggled the ear of the dirt-stained stuffed dog clutched in Zoe's arms. "Who's this?"

"Misser Peabody."

"I heard that somebody found Mister Peabody for you after the storm. Where did they find him?"

"He was stuck in a 'lectric wire high, high over the trees. On TV, they showed a pitcher of him stuck, and my mom called, and a man from the 'lectric company climbed up and got him and bringed him to me."

April stood with her hand on the little girl's shoulder and faced the camera. "Just one of hundreds of stories we've heard in the past few days, which is why KXPB is joining forces with local churches, businesses, and organizations to help raise funds for these families and. . . ."

"She's a natural."

Seth jumped at the out-of-place voice. "Gil! What are you doing here?"

Gil Cadwell ran a hand through his hair. "I hope I'm here to bring you some peace."

No words came to mind. Seth settled for a raise of his eyebrows.

"I had a little talk with my daughter the other day." His eyes sparkled with mirth. "I informed her that I had no record of her paying off her credit card debt to me."

"What?" Seth couldn't believe what he was hearing. This was the man Brenda called "Old Softy" to his face.

"Yup. It felt awfully good, too. You should have seen the look on Margaret's face when I calmly stated that there were no papers that indicated that the monetary gifts Seth Bachelor had been sending me for the past three years had anything to do with what Brenda owed me." Gil winked and chuckled. "I said that I would, however, be willing to expunge her debt if she signed over her half of the station to you, no strings attached." He pulled an envelope from his jacket pocket and handed it to Seth. "Be happy, son."

❧

"Are you sure I'm not stepping on some reporter's toes?" Picking her way along a sidewalk strewn with debris, April handed the microphone to Seth. "Is this really okay with your boss?"

"I. . .don't have a boss."

A sick feeling settled hard in April's stomach. Had he gotten in another argument? Or gotten fired for taking off last Friday? "You lost your job?"

The granddaddy of all patronizing expressions swept over Seth's face.

Men! Why had she ever tried to understand this one? "What happened?"

"I don't have a boss, but I do have a job. More of one than I want, actually."

She was too tired for games. She'd spent most of the past

week serving meals and reading stories to children at the emergency shelters set up in three church basements. . .and doing television interviews of the victims. This was the fifth day that her coverage would be broadcast on the six o'clock news, yet she still hadn't spoken to anyone at KXPB other than Seth and the cameraman. The whole setup struck her as odd. But she loved every exhausted minute of it. It didn't matter that she had no idea if she'd be compensated for her reporting time. The thought had occurred to her more than once that, if she'd still been working at KPOG, she wouldn't have been freed up to do this. God was in control. Raising public awareness of the needs of these people who were truly homeless was where she was supposed to be. And by the time she dropped onto Yvonne's couch around midnight every night, she was too worn-out to feel the lumpy cushions.

She aimed a lopsided smile at Seth. "I'm too brain-dead for riddles, Mr. Bachelor. Spit it out."

He handed the microphone to the cameraman. His hands rested on her shoulders, and he kissed the tip of her nose. "We need to talk."

"That sounds ominous."

"I hope it's not." His hand slid over hers, and they walked toward the road.

An elderly couple who April had interviewed earlier in the week stood beside a washer and dryer, the only things still intact in the pile of tinder that had once been their home. April waved, and the man held up a sheaf of crumpled papers. "We found our marriage license!"

His wife laughed. "We're still legal!"

"Congratulations!" April turned to Seth. "Why does it take losing everything to figure out what's really important?"

Brown eyes smiled back at her. "What have you figured out so far?"

"That God's plans don't have to make sense." She grinned

at him. "And men don't either."

He laughed. "Thank you. That makes this next part so much easier."

"You're scaring me."

"Just hear me out. This is one of those Lots of Grace Required moments."

"O. . .kay."

Seth steered her around a dented microwave on the side of the road. "I haven't been completely. . .forthright about some things, and I'm hoping my reasons will make sense." He took an audible deep breath. "A few days before our wedding date, Brenda's father gave us a wedding gift. An unbelievable wedding gift."

He stopped to say hi to two men from the power company, giving April's imagination time to spin out of control.

"He deeded KXPB and his helicopter to the two of us."

"You *own* the station?" April stopped walking. "With Brenda?"

"I did. Until half an hour ago. That was her father I was talking to." Seth rubbed the back of his neck. "I made a deal with Brenda, a stupid deal, in retrospect. She didn't want to sell me her half of the station. Looking back, I realize I should have just walked away from it, but I offered to pay off her credit card debt and the debt to her father in payment for my half of the station. I didn't have a thing put in writing. I love her dad and trust him implicitly. I figured that with him involved she wouldn't try anything underhanded. But when I made my last payment, she refused to sign the deed over to me. Anyway. . .Daddy stepped in, and the deed is now in my name alone."

April's knees felt like jelly, like the feeling after a near miss on the freeway. "You *own* the station?"

"And my second order of business will be to fire my station manager, which will make me the temporary manager as well as owner." A sheepish look spread across his face. "I'm the man upstairs."

April's mouth opened, but what came out wasn't indignation. It was laughter. "You're the one who didn't hire me because I might move on?"

"Kind of ironic, isn't it?" His fingertips pulled a strand of hair off her cheek. "But I'd like to make amends for that mistake. I've been wanting to for weeks. That's the reason I shared your talk show idea with Brenda."

"I'm guessing she wasn't all in favor of the idea." An almost literal light went on in April's consciousness. "She's still in love with you! That's why she tried to get me away from here, isn't it? That's why she was so willing to join forces with my mother."

Seth's gaze dropped to the ground. "Apparently."

Rising on tiptoes, she brushed her lips across his forehead. "Who could blame her?"

He smiled, clearly relieved that she'd broken the tension. "Anyway, the strings are all cut, and I'm free to make executive decisions. So the first one I'm making is to offer you a daily talk show. Real people, real stories, with a real beautiful host. Interested?"

At that moment, KXPB's newly hired talk show host couldn't have put two words together if her life depended on it. Her tears answered for her.

twenty-one

"Thank you, John." April smiled at John Nelson, Pine Bluff's town chairman, sitting across from her in an overstuffed leather chair. Turning toward Camera Two, she was glad she couldn't see beyond the lights, or her gaze would have strayed to the man with dark brown eyes. The man who, every week for ten months now, had watched her from his chair beside the studio door. "Tomorrow night we'll be talking to Trace and Sydney McKay—a real-life 'prison to praise' story. Thanks for joining us."

April uncrossed her legs, shedding the tension that came with taping a show. "That was an amazing story, John. After this airs tonight, we'll get tons of e-mail."

Leaning forward and resting his elbows on his knees, John gave her a strange look. "You know, my heart attack not only brought me to Christ, it also left me with an insatiable desire to experience things I'd never done before. Legal things—not like climbing a water tower." He winked at April.

"This sounds like a topic for another show. What kind of things?" April picked up the water bottle that sat on the floor beside her chair.

"Hot air ballooning, for one. I wanted to try it, just once. But being up there, away from all the hustle and bustle, seeing this panorama of God's handiwork, I got hooked. The experience is. . .worship. That's the only way I can describe it. Especially right now with the trees all in bloom. So I got trained, and I bought a share in a balloon. I'm giving rides to everyone I know. Including you."

"It is on my list, John. Someday. . ."

"Today's as good as any. Gorgeous spring day and the air's still. Right about sundown would be perfect. Let's go."

As April responded with a nervous chuckle, Seth stepped out of the dark, holding out her jacket and a wrapped package, shoe box size. Only then did she notice the cameras were still on.

❧

John cranked the burner, and April's fingers bit into the side of the wicker basket. Anticipating a stomach-lurching sensation at liftoff, she closed her eyes and buried her face in Seth's shoulder.

"Smile for the camera." His breath was warm on her cheek.

"I can't. Tell me when we're off the ground."

"We're off the ground."

"What?" Now that she concentrated on it, she could sense that the earth was no longer beneath her feet. Cautiously, she opened her eyes. The ground crew waved, a KXPB camera tilted up to track them. The figures grew small. A burst of noise drew her eyes to the flame spurting from the burner and the envelope of primary colors that towered overhead. "Amazing."

Pine Bluff and the St. Croix shrank beneath their feet as they drifted northwest on the air currents. April pointed out Main Street and the chamber of commerce building. Seth found his house. Soft pinks, luminous purples, and stark whites dotted the spaces between houses. In seconds, they were at eye level to the catwalk on the water tower.

Seth pointed toward the tower. "Remember a year ago when we shared a moment at the top of that thing?"

"I'll never forget it. Believe me, I've tried." Still gripping the side of the basket, she grinned up at him.

"Maybe I can make a moment you'll want to remember."

"You already are."

Seth bent down and picked up the box he'd taunted her with since they'd left the studio. "Now you can open it."

April turned slowly and anchored her back against the side. Behind Seth, John winked and turned away from them. Tearing through the paper, she handed the crumpled wads to Seth and lifted the cover. Two things sat side by side in the box. A book and a hat.

"It's a Mary hat!"

Seth took the tam out of the box and set it on her head. "I thought you might need something to throw from up here."

Leaning over the box, she took his face in both hands and kissed him. "I love you."

"Because of a measly old hat?" He reached into the box and turned over the thick, spiral-bound book.

Block lettering across the pale green cover spelled out "April's Dream List."

"I thought it was time you made your own list." He pulled a pen from his shirt pocket. "And I was kind of hoping I could be on it."

Wiping a tear from the book's cover and another from her chin, April shook her head. "You already are." Taking the pen, she opened the book. . .and her mouth. The shoe box clattered to the basket floor.

A hole had been meticulously cut through the blank pages. And a small black box nestled in the space. With shaking fingers, she lifted the box and then held it out for Seth to open.

The setting sun glinted off the square diamond and the two little emeralds beside it.

"I love you, April Jean, and I want to spend the rest of my life sharing adventures with you."

Smiling through tears, April held out her left hand. "That wasn't a question, but the answer is yes." He slid the ring on, and she raised her hand to the peach pink sun. "You won't be a bachelor anymore."

"No." His arms slipped around her. "But you will be."

Laughing, she leaned into him. "Know what?"

"What?"

"I don't think I'm afraid of heights anymore."

❧

Behind Pastor Owen, the stone chimney stretched to the vaulted ceiling of the rustic lodge. Flames crackled in the hearth, adding their rhythm to the chords of two acoustic guitars. Outside the windows, red and white pines stood guard and quaking aspen leaves rattled in the September breeze.

April stared down at the silver band that nested with her engagement ring and then up at the man who had just placed it there. She willed the tears that balanced on her lower lashes not to fall on the white satin that rippled at her feet.

Pastor Owen raised his hands. "Ladies and gentlemen, it is my honor and pleasure to introduce to you Mr. and Mrs. Seth Bachelor."

Over the applause, "Ode to Joy" rose from the guitars. As Yvonne handed her bouquet back to her, she whispered, "I told you so."

"You sure did."

Seth took her hand, and they walked down the aisle.

When they reached the back, Yvonne, in floor-length rust-colored satin, took Darren's arm and walked toward them, blowing a kiss to her husband as she passed him.

Tissue wadded in one hand, the other swiping at tears, April's mother, looking stronger than she had in years, held her arms out to Seth first. She kissed her son-in-law on the cheek and turned to April. "Thank you, honey."

"For what?"

"For forgiving my meddling. And for ignoring my advice."

As her mother walked away, April allowed a few brief seconds to scan the reception line, looking for her father. She wasn't surprised he hadn't come.

Seth's parents were next. Rod Bachelor hugged his son in a

gesture that didn't seem natural, but his smile seemed genuine. "We'll set four places for Christmas dinner this year." His wife nodded and kissed April on the cheek.

Denisha, holding the hand of a toddling girl in head-to-toe pink, prodded Wesley toward April. "He's having some problems with this big change. He needs some reassurance from you two."

Large brown eyes looked up at Seth. "Is there still gonna be Man Room?"

Seth squatted down to Wesley's level. "Absolutely. Your mom and April and baby Grace will stay in the kitchen where they belong."

A smile split Wesley's face. "That's Girl Room, isn't it?"

In spite of the toe of April's shoe connecting with his leg, Seth laughed. "It sure is."

Another furrow creased the boy's brow as he looked up at April. "Are you gonna be in Daddy and Uncle Seth's comp'ny and chase storms now?"

Seth's face turned up expectantly. "Now there's a good question."

April's eyebrow rose. "You know what? I just might."

"So you're not scared anymore?"

"Oh, I'm still scared. But being brave means doing things even when you're scared."

April hugged friends from college, coworkers, Seth's relatives, and neighbors from her childhood. And then Jill stood before her, tears in her eyes, her manicured nails sweeping along the lines of April's pearl-trimmed gown. "I think you've finally reached your full potential, girl. You look beautiful."

When they'd shaken the last hand and the guests had moved into the dining room, Midge stood alone, facing the fireplace. April walked across the room. "Midge? Are you okay?"

Her aunt's hairsprayed curls bobbed in affirmation, but it

took her a moment to turn around. Eyes red, lashes smudged, Midge smiled. "I have something for you." She opened her lavender purse and pulled out a tissue. "Here, you'll need this." The next thing to come out of the clutch was an envelope. "I've been holding on to this for almost two years."

April's name was written on the front. In Caitlyn's handwriting.

Midge walked away, and Seth's arm slid around April's shoulders as she opened the envelope.

Hey Ape,

So this is the big day, huh? The one we always dreamed of. I'm so sorry I can't be there, standing by your side, making you laugh so your mascara doesn't run. Knowing how picky you are, this guy must be amazing. I know you wouldn't settle for anyone who didn't make you feel totally loved and safe and protected. After all you've been through, you deserve that. While you're floating on his arm tonight, think of me, but do it with a smile. I'm dancing with The Bridegroom now.

Love you forever,
Cait

Seth held her until her tears stopped and then took the tissue and wiped her face. "So, Mrs. Bachelor, what's next on your dream list?"

Standing on tiptoes, she brushed her lips against his cheek. "Just you."

A Letter To Our Readers

Dear Reader:
In order that we might better contribute to your reading enjoyment, we would appreciate your taking a few minutes to respond to the following questions. We welcome your comments and read each form and letter we receive. When completed, please return to the following:

Fiction Editor
Heartsong Presents
PO Box 719
Uhrichsville, Ohio 44683

1. Did you enjoy reading *Dream Chasers* by Becky Melby and Cathy Wienke?
   ❏ Very much! I would like to see more books by this author!
   ❏ Moderately. I would have enjoyed it more if

   _____

   _____

   _____

2. Are you a member of **Heartsong Presents**? ❏ Yes ❏ No
   If no, where did you purchase this book? _____

   _____

3. How would you rate, on a scale from 1 (poor) to 5 (superior), the cover design? _____

4. On a scale from 1 (poor) to 10 (superior), please rate the following elements.

   ____ Heroine   ____ Plot
   ____ Hero   ____ Inspirational theme
   ____ Setting   ____ Secondary characters

5. These characters were special because? _____
_____
_____

6. How has this book inspired your life? _____
_____
_____

7. What settings would you like to see covered in future
   Heartsong Presents books? _____
_____
_____

8. What are some inspirational themes you would like to see
   treated in future books? _____
_____
_____

9. Would you be interested in reading other **Heartsong
   Presents** titles? ❏ Yes ❏ No

10. Please check your age range:
    ❏ Under 18   ❏ 18-24
    ❏ 25-34   ❏ 35-45
    ❏ 46-55   ❏ Over 55

Name _____
Occupation _____
Address _____
City, State, Zip _____

STAND-IN

*G*ROOM

When professional wedding planner Anne Hawthorne first meets the handsome Englishman George Laurence, she wonders if God has finally answered her prayers for a husband. But when the "best man" for her turns out to be a client—and someone else's to-have-and-to-hold—Anne quickly realizes that planning his wedding will be no honeymoon. Can she remain professional while falling for the groom?

Contemporary, paperback, 304 pages, 5³/₁₆" x 8"

Please send me ____ copies of *Stand-In Groom*. I am enclosing $10.97 for each.
(Please add $4.00 to cover postage and handling per order. OH add 7% tax.
If outside the U.S. please call 740-922-7280 for shipping charges.)

Name_____

Address _____

City, State, Zip _____

Heart♥ng

Any 12
Heartsong
Presents titles
for only
$27.00*

CONTEMPORARY ROMANCE IS CHEAPER BY THE DOZEN!
Buy any assortment of twelve *Heartsong Presents* titles and save 25% off the already discounted price of $2.97 each!

*plus $4.00 shipping and handling per order and sales tax where applicable.
If outside the U.S. please call 740-922-7280 for shipping charges.

HEARTSONG PRESENTS TITLES AVAILABLE NOW:

(If ordering from this page, please remember to include it with the order form.)

Presents